MW01229662

Sink The Zinc

By: Terri Talley Venters

An Elements Of Mystery Book

Sink The Zinc ©2020 by Terri Talley Venters

Cover illustration © 2020
For information on the cover art, please contact Valerie
Tibbs

All rights reserved. No part of this book may be reproduced
or transmitted in any form without written permission
from the publisher, except by a reviewer who may quote
brief passages for review purposes. If you are reading this
book and did not buy it or win it in a contest by the author,
publisher, or authorized distributor, you are reading an
illegal copy. This hurts the author and publisher. Please
delete and purchase a legal copy from one of its
distributors.

Although inspired by true events, this book is a work of
fiction and any resemblance to any person, living or dead,
any place, events or occurrences, is purely coincidental.
The characters and story lines are created from the
author's imagination or are used fictitiously.

Editor: Leslie S. Talley

Print ISBN 9798592399077

If you are interested in purchasing more works of this
nature, please stop by www.ElementsOfMystery.com.
Printed in The United States of America

Sharing any electronic file without the copyright holder or
publisher's permission is illegal and subject to a fine of up
to $250,000.

Elements of Mystery Books

By:
Terri Talley Venters

Carbon Copy Saga
Carbon Copy
Tin Roof
Silver Lining
Luke's Lithium

Cauldron Series
Copper Cauldron
Cobalt Cauldron
Calcium Cauldron
Chromium Cauldron
Zirconium Cauldron

Under The Magic Adventures
Sulfur Springs
Europium Gem Mine
Noah's Nickel
Manganese Magic
Platinum Princess
Plutonium Princess

Stand Alone Novels
Iron Curtains
Body Of Gold
Elements of Mystery
Hidden Helium
Under The Magic Collection
Sink The Zinc

Dedication

—To my father, Luther Talley, and my youngest niece, Leila Talley, for whom the main characters in this book are named.

Prologue

1061 days before first human dies of 61-DIVOC

"I can't believe you just sweet talked our way into Le Cellier Steakhouse on Valentine's Day without a reservation." Luke smiled at his wife of nearly 23 years. Not a single fleck of gray shone on his full head of sandy-blond hair. His sea-green eyes stood out with his blue, Florida Gator golf shirt.

"You can't get it if you don't ask." Leila smiled flirtatiously at Luke as a Cast Member escorted them into their favorite restaurant in EPCOT. She chose a light-blue dress to accentuate her baby-blue eyes and long, blonde hair.

"Guess what I'll ask for back at the room later?" Luke playfully smacked her bottom.

The Cast Member placed their menus on the table and said, "Welcome to Le Cellier. Gloria, your server, will be with you momentarily. Have a 'Magical Day.'"

"Isn't Valentine's Day always a sure thing? Like birthdays and anniversaries?" She slid into their favorite booth in the back of the restaurant.

"Every day with you is like Valentine's Day." He squinted as he studied the menu in the dimly lit restaurant.

"Why study the menu? Don't we always get the same thing?" she referred to their scrumptious filet mignon on top of mushroom risotto.

"I know, but I'm curious about the appetizers. Steak tartare. That's new," he said.

"Steak before steak? How about the cheese plate?" she asked while studying the extensive wine list.

Another Cast Member arrived and said, "Welcome to Le Cellier. My name is Gloria. Have you dined with us before?"

Leila and Luke nodded in unison.

"Great, then you know our restaurant is divided into twelve separate territories, just like Canada. You're seated in the British Columbia Territory. Will you be using any dining plans this evening?" she asked.

"Tables of Wonderland," Leila referred to their discount card which gave them 20% off their entire meal, including alcohol. They normally recouped the price of the annual card in one weekend. As annual passholders for over twenty years, they frequently drove down to Disney from Jacksonville, Florida. Usually their teenage sons accompanied them, but tonight they enjoyed a rare date night.

"Excellent. Can I start you off with a bottle of wine or an appetizer?" Gloria asked.

Luke gestured towards Leila to allow her to order whatever she wanted.

Pointing to her wine selection, she said, "We'll have a bottle of this Bordeaux and the Artisan Cheese Plate." Leila placed the wine menu down and mentally salivated over their imminent feast.

Gloria scurried off to fetch their wine and cheese plate.

Luke grabbed Leila's hand from across the table and smiled. "Oh, I bought our tickets to the Metallica concert. I joined the fan club which allowed me to preorder a day early. I bought four great seats and put two tickets up for sale for twice what I paid. We're basically seeing Metallica for free."

"Nothing says I love you on Valentine's Day like Metallica tickets." Leila grinned.

"Or matching 357s," Luke referred to their Christmas presents to each other. This particular handgun shot both .38 and .357 caliber bullets. He'd prepared for the Apocalypse/Armageddon for years.

Guns and ammunition proved essential to survive the end of days.

Gloria appeared with a smile and a bottle of Bordeaux. She presented the bottle to them, and they eagerly nodded their approval. She uncorked the wine and poured Leila a sample.

Leila went through the proper wine tasting routine of twirling the glass to study the viscosity of the legs as they slipped down the inner part of the glass, then she sniffed the aroma before tasting the bold goodness of the heavy Bordeaux. "Mmmm."

Gloria poured a few ounces of wine into their oversized goblets. "Your cheese plate should arrive momentarily. Ready to order?"

Luke said, "We'll both have filet mignon, medium rare."

"Excellent choice," Gloria said as a food runner delivered their cheese plate.

"Happy Valentine's Day." Luke lifted his glass and toasted Leila's.

"Happy Valentine's Day." She drank her wine and hummed. "What's next on the 'prepare for the Apocalypse to-do list?'" As a best-selling author, Leila's overactive imagination always spun wild theories about the end of the world—zombie apocalypse, global warming melting the glaciers and flooding the world, bees going extinct and the world running out of food, solar flares scorching humans to death, aliens invading, overpopulation depleting natural resources and humans becoming extinct, or some new virus causing a pandemic.

"I plan to build a few raised vegetable gardens to grow vegetables and lettuce," Luke said.

"Grow potatoes. It's the only food which provides all the nutrients humans need to survive." Leila took a bite of smoked Canadian cheddar cheese.

"I'm growing tons of herbs for cooking—rosemary, thyme, basil, dill, cilantro, mint and parsley. But I'd like to grow medicinal herbs, too. Luckily, we live on the river and can catch fish and shoot those annoying Canadian Geese if the world runs out of food," Luke said.

"Shhh. Don't forget, we're in Canada," Leila scolded.

"'Dope.'" Luke impersonated Homer Simpson.

"Since we live next to the woods, we'll have plenty of firewood to cook our food. Since our cats hunt, they'll survive on lizards and birds."

"At least we're prepared to survive the Apocalypse." He sipped wine.

Leila laughed. "We'll know the world is ending when Disney closes!"

Chapter One

101 days before first human dies of 61-DIVOC

The President of the United States of America, Alexander Ace, sat behind his desk in the Oval Office and fired off a tweet from his iPhone. As he tapped away, he chuckled to himself. *The Fake News will have a field day with this one.*

"Excuse me, Mr. President, the Secretary of Defense is waiting to see you," Ericka, the Chief of Staff, said.

"Send him in," President Ace said as he pocketed his iPhone. With perfectly coiffed and heavily sprayed blond hair parted on the left, he wore a navy-blue suit, white shirt and red silk tie.

The Secretary of Defense, also a Five-Star Fleet Admiral, entered wearing navy dress blues and saluted the POTUS. "Mr. President."

"Secretary Lucas." President Ace stood to his six-foot, three-inch height and shook Lucas's hand.

"I have an urgent report that's so important I must hand it to you directly." Lucas handed President Ace a file labeled—TOP SECRET.

President Ace grabbed the file, sat back down and opened it. A typed report accompanied several photographs. Incredulous, he read the Top-Secret report as his mind processed the ramifications for not only the American People, but the entire Human Race.

Being a successful business man, he got straight to the point. "How much time do we have?" President Ace asked without changing his normal, pouty-lipped expression.

"Almost eight months," Lucas said.

"Who else knows about this?" President Ace asked.

"Just the top guys at NASA. All communication related to this matter of national security is old school. No computers, internet or phones. Only hand delivered, manually typed memos. And only secure face-to-face conversations."

"No other country knows?" President Ace asked.

"There's no indication that another country knows. Our technology and resources are far superior. NSA hasn't picked up even a whisper about this."

"I hope you're right because China likes to hide important stuff from us. They lie to us, steal our technology, infiltrate our universities and spy on us. That's not racist or xenophobic, that's a proven fact," the President said matter-of-factly.

"Yes, Mr. President."

"Where are these coordinates?" President Ace stood and approached the spinning globe in his Oval office. He studied the Latitude and Longitude lines on the globe and ran his finger to their intersection on the globe. "Not America, that's fantastic. Very few people at this particular location, also fantastic." But the ramifications of this particular location sank in.

"Now I understand why NASA went directly to you first. I assume you have a plan to save as many Americans as possible?" President Ace asked.

Lucas nodded and explained his plan.

"Fantastic plan. We obviously cannot tell the world about this," President Ace said.

"I couldn't agree more, Mr. President. Telling the world would create mass hysteria. They'd destroy each other long before eight months from now. Do we let the people we can't save continue on business as usual?" Lucas asked.

"No, we want them to spend their last months on Earth at home with their families," President Ace said.

"How do we get Americans to stay home with their families without telling them the truth?" Lucas asked.

President Ace said, "We start a pandemic."

Chapter Two

11 days before first human dies of 61-DIVOC

"Can we stay up until Midnight?" Leila asked Andrea, her BFF since high school.

"We'll definitely pass out way before then." Andrea raised her nearly empty wine glass to Leila and toasted, "Cheers."

Leila and Andrea, along with their husbands, usually celebrated New Year's Eve together. Their annual tradition included a delicious, home cooked meal paired with lots of alcohol and laughter. They alternated hosting at their respective homes. This year, they celebrated at Leila and Luke's home on the Saint John's River in Jacksonville.

Leila and Andrea sat on the patio overlooking the river with a great view of the Dames Point Bridge.

"I loved those Kobe beef sliders with Brie." Andrea rubbed her belly and placed her empty wine glass on the side table.

Leila noticed the empty glass and hollered at her two teenage sons who fished in the river. "Boys, can one of you please fill Aunt Andrea's wine glass?" Although not biologically related, they considered Andrea and Scott part of the family.

"Uncle Damon gives us a dollar every time we get him a beer," Zach said.

"No wonder you're so rich," Leila retorted. Then she wrangled her tangential thoughts back to dinner. "Luke recreated those sliders from one of our favorite Happy Hour places. If you sit in the lounge at Matthew's Restaurant, they offer $5 house wines and $5 small plates. One of the small plates is sliders. Matthew also owns M Shack and knows how to cook a tasty burger."

"Mmm, Chef Big Boy knows how to cook, too!" Andrea referred to Luke's nickname used by everybody except Leila. Although nearly six-feet tall with a slender physique, Luke's nickname somehow stuck. "What are Big Boy and Scott doing?"

"Luke's probably showing off his arsenal and Armageddon supplies." Leila rolled her eyes at her husband's over preparedness. But he and their sons are Eagle Scouts, after all. 'Be prepared.'

Zach appeared with a bottle of wine and presented it to Andrea like a Wine Sommelier at a fancy restaurant. He uncorked the bottle and refilled their glasses.

"Thanks, Zach." Andrea turned to Leila and asked. Do you always drink this much in front of your boys? Do you think it's a bad influence?"

"Yes and no. We teach them responsible drinking. We drink at home, after 5 and don't drive. In fact, now that they're old enough to drive, they are our designated drivers if we eat out or attend a family gathering. In fact, the boys sometimes drive their grandpa and uncle," Leila explained.

"Smart. I'm ready to play a board game," Andrea said.

"David, can you please bring us Cards Against Humanity?" Leila asked.

"Mom, I'm not playing that game with ya'll. You just don't get it." David rolled his eyes like an annoyed teenager.

"I don't remember inviting you," Leila retorted.

Leila, Andrea, Scott and Luke sat at the round mahogany kitchen table and played Cards Against Humanity.

"I'm surprised that ya'll didn't take a big trip for your 25th wedding anniversary." Andrea said while studying her white cards.

"We wanted to go to Scandinavia in June, but Luke couldn't get away from the Cape Project for that long. Then we hoped to take the boys to Italy and Spain for Christmas and see many of our former exchange students. Scandinavia is way too cold in the winter. But then David needed minor surgery, and we scheduled it during Christmas break so he wouldn't miss school. He got straight A's his first semester at UCF!" Leila loved to brag about her awesome sons. She epitomized a proud mamma bear.

"They say, things happen for a reason. It's your destiny to spend New Year's Eve at home instead of bouncing all over Europe.

Bzzzzzzzz

Bzzzzzzzz

Bzzzzzzzz

Bzzzzzzzz

All of their smart phones buzzed simultaneously

WAOK News Alert
Chinese authorities treat dozens of pneumonia cases of unknown causes

"Scott, didn't you have a bad case of pneumonia a few years ago?" Leila asked.

"Yes, ten years ago. I spent 8 days in the hospital. That's how I quit smoking," Scott said.

Leila and Luke shot judgmental scowls to Andrea who'd smoked since thirteen.

Andrea threw her hands up in the air and said, "I know, I need to quit. What do you think caused all of these pneumonia cases?" she asked, changing the subject.

Leila shrugged, "Who knows what China hides from us."

Chapter Three

0 days before first human dies of 61-DIVOC

"Zach, David, come here, quick!" Luke hollered for his sons to come downstairs.

"What Dad? It's Saturday, we're trying to sleep," Zach whined from the second floor.

David and Zach begrudgingly walked downstairs. Zach wore Home Alone flannel pajama bottoms which read—'You filthy animal.' Shirtless, he flexed his eight-pack abs. David wore a white, long-sleeve Guns and Roses shirt and flannel pajama bottoms which read Dunder Mifflin from the hit television series—*The Office.*

"Grab every Ace thing you own and meet me outside," Luke said.

"What's this?" Leila asked.

"I'm entering a contest." Luke beamed excitedly.

"You're always entering a contest. You devote your Saturday mornings to it." Leila poured a cup of green tea into her oversized Minnie Mouse mug.

"Leila, can you please turn Zach's car around in the driveway so we can see his Ace New York plate on the front of his car?" Luke asked, then took another sip of espresso.

"Sure, but why?" Leila asked.

"You'll see." Luke grinned excitedly.

Leila grabbed Zach's spare Elantra keys from the junk drawer, walked out the front door and moved the silver car around.

The boys walked outside donning their Ace paraphernalia. Zach wore a red Ace 2020 bucket hat, red Ace 'Keep America Great' tee shirt and red 'Make America Great Again' socks. David wore a red Ace 'Keep America Great' baseball cap and an Ace tee shirt. This shirt showed a picture of President Ace, President Osama and President Willy. Next to the picture of President Ace, it read—More Jobs. Next to the picture of President Osama, it read—No Jobs. And next to the picture of President Willy, it read—Blow Jobs.

"What kind of contest?" Leila asked as she exited the car.

"A chance to win a free weekend with President Ace at Ace Cay," Luke referred President's palace on a private island in Florida.

"No way! That sounds awesome! Now the Ace gear makes sense. What's involved in the contest?" Leila asked.

"We just tweet a picture with hashtag #ACE2020," Luke said.

"That sounds easy. Boys, stand in front of the car and hold up the flag. Make sure we can see the gold front license plate—Ace New York." Luke referred to the front license plate Zach purchased on a recent trip to New York City.

"Now, hold up the flag between ya'll." Luke referred to David's flag with a picture of President Ace, the American Flag and the caption—Ace 2020 No More Bullshit.

"Awesome guys," Leila said proudly. Both of her sons decided on their own that they supported President Ace. In fact, David and Zach planned to vote for Ace in the November Election. She'd raised them right.

Luke snapped a few pictures on his iPhone X and studied them. Appearing impressed, he gave the boys a thumbs up.

"I wanna see." Leila walked over to Luke and studied the first image on his iPhone.

Luke slid the images across the screen.

"Wow! They're actually smiling," Leila said incredulously as she admired the images of her handsome sons and pointed at her favorite picture. "That's the one."

Luke uploaded the picture onto Twitter and tweeted #Ace2020. "Done."

"When is the trip? Assuming we win, of course." Leila epitomized optimism.

"May 4th."

"Star Wars Day." Leila referred to the day Star Wars fans proclaimed May the *Fourth* because phonetically it sounded similar to the famous lines from all of the Star Wars Movies—'May the *Force* be with you.'

Bzzzzzz

Bzzzzzz

They studied their iPhones simultaneously.

WAOK News Alert
First Human dies in China from 61-DIVOC

Chapter Four

10 days after first human dies of 61-DIVOC

Leila uncorked a bottle of Chianti, poured a glass, and then sipped the bold goodness. *Mmmmm.* She turned on the television to watch *The Truth* on WAOK News.

She enjoyed this show because they made fun of the Democrats and joked about their hypocrisy and Fake News. While listening to the news casters banter, news bands scrolled across the bottom of the television screen.

Confirmed cases of 61-DIVOC reported in Japan, South Korea and Thailand
Wuhoo Provence cut off by Chinese authorities to stop the spread of the virus
United States reported its first confirmed case in Washington State of a man who recently returned from Wuhoo

"Oh, you're home." Leila turned to Luke who sweetly pecked her lips.

"Mom, what's for dinner?" Zach asked from the upstairs loft.

"Chicken Parm," Leila hollered.

"Yes," Zach said excitedly, a rare moment for a teenager.

"Turn the television off. Bad news upsets you," Luke said.

"That's why I poured a glass of wine first." She held up her glass. "Speaking of which, let me pour you a glass while we prep dinner."

Leila poured Luke a glass of wine and handed it to him. "Cheers."

"Cheers." Luke sipped wine and opened the Pandora app on his iPhone. He pressed the cast button and Depeche Mode's hit song, *Personal Jesus,* resonated throughout the sound system.

Leila grated parmigiana cheese while sipping wine and enjoying 80's music. She recalled attending a Depeche Mode concert in 2013 and relived the happy memory of a fantastic show.

Luke nodded towards the television. "Is the world about to end? Will we need our Armageddon supplies?" Luke asked while he pounded a chicken breast. Their Black Persian cat, Sabbath, jumped onto the 'cooking chair' and patiently awaited his imminent feast of raw meat. As a kitten, Sabbath always circled Luke's ankles during dinner prep. Concerned about stepping on the tiny furball, Luke moved a chair to the end of the counter which allowed Sabbath to safely watch the action and receive scraps of raw meat.

"The Stock Market seems to think so, we lost money today." Leila cringed. Her disciplined savings and diligent investing had skyrocketed their accounts over the years, especially since their beloved President Ace took office. But with the uncertainty of a potential pandemic, the Stock Market declined daily.

"Can you boil the pasta water?" Luke asked. "My fingers are covered in raw chicken."

"Speaking of raw meat, I heard this whole virus started because some bizarre wet market in Wuhoo served raw monkey brains to tourists as a delicacy. Supposedly, they served the brains in the monkey's skull." Leila cringed at the nasty notion.

"Something weird is happening." Luke shook his head as he dipped a raw chicken breast into the battered eggs before dusting it with breadcrumbs.

"What? Do you think the Chinese started this virus intentionally?" she asked. Her imagination ran wild.

"You and your conspiracy theories." He shook his head incredulously.

She sipped wine and shrugged nonchalantly. "What can I say? I have an overactive imagination. It's an occupational hazard."

"But you're a CPA," he retorted.

"That's just my day job. I'm talking about my novel writing hobby." She filled the large pot with water, placed it onto the cooktop stove and turned the heat on.

"I'd hardly call writing multiple New York Times Bestsellers a hobby," Luke referred to her huge success as a fiction novelist.

She changed the subject. "Why would China start a virus in their own country? Unless they're trying to reduce overpopulation," Leila speculated.

Luke shrugged as he washed his hands.

"Maybe they want to ruin our economy so Ace won't get re-elected. China hates President Ace because he makes America better and China worse," Leila speculated.

Luke shrugged again.

Leila moved the shredded parmesan cheese onto the kitchen island next to the cooktop stove. She looked out at the river and watched a big cargo ship dock at the Blunt Island Terminal to unload thousands of foreign cars. "If China wanted to infect us, why wouldn't they just infect all those cars they export?"

"Those cars are Japanese," he corrected.

"Close enough," she quipped as she cut onions for the salad. "What are you so worried about?"

With a doom's day tone of voice, Luke said, "I've *really* got a bad feeling about this!"

Sink The Zinc

Chapter Five

31 days after first human dies of 61-DIVOC

"More of your crap arrived today," Leila said. Everyday more and more Amazon Prime packages arrived on their doorstep.

Luke said defensively, "Hey, we need all this crap to survive Armageddon. I ordered zinc and vitamin C to boost our immune systems. But Amazon limits the quantity because there's a shortage."

"What's in that big box?" she asked, a little miffed that so many boxes filled her beautiful foyer.

"Cool. That must be my rain barrel. I'll divert water from the rain gutters. One rain storm will fill that thing in seconds." Luke snapped his fingers.

Leila poured two glasses of wine, handed one to Luke and said, "Cheers."

"At least the rain barrel is useful. Now we won't have to worry about buying water and filling the bathtub every time a hurricane comes," he rationalized a portion of his exorbitant spending preparing for the end of the world. I can connect the hose to the rain barrel's spout and water my garden for free." Luke loved his amazing garden.

"Speaking of free. I'm about to use our Disney dollars. I booked two trips to Disney and got a great deal at the Pop Century Resort. That's one of the hotels that you can ride the new Skyliner from the hotel to EPCOT and Hollywood Studios."

"Two trips?" Luke asked as he fried garlic to accompany their sautéed spinach.

"Yes, I actually convinced David to spend three days of his spring break with me. Then the following week, I'm taking my nieces to Disney. Malia, Leila and Rebecca have annual passes, too. The girls excitedly predicted, 'the best spring break ever'. I'm not sure who is more excited about the Disney trip—them or me," she said.

"Definitely you." He swallowed a healthy gulp of wine.

Leila turned on the television to *The Truth* on WAOK News. She sipped wine and studied the statistics on the television screen.

The death toll in China reached 1,113
Total number of confirmed cases rose to 44,653
393 cases reported outside of China
24 countries reported 61-DIVOC cases

"Holy shit! Are you seeing this? This virus spreads fast. I have a bad feeling that you're right about this leading to the end of the world." Leila swallowed a big gulp of wine to calm her nerves. She got up during the commercial break to set the table and heat up the polenta.

"I told you I've got a really bad feeling about this. I talked to this guy at work and figured out what kind of AR-15 to buy," Luke said.

"Oh, good. Order it up before all the guns sell out," she said.

"Funny you said that. I stopped by Academy Sports on my way home and thought they stopped selling guns because only a few guns occupied the display cases. Turns out, guns sell out within hours of delivery," he said as he grilled marinated chicken breasts.

"Maybe I should buy stock in Smith & Wesson. Speaking of stock, I sold about $100,000 of our stocks today and I cashed in our capital gains. Our E*Trade accounts grew over 40% since President Ace won the 2016 Election. I freed up some cash in case the shit hits the fan. Plus, I know the Stock Market will tank once the cooties invade the United States. I plan to buy back stocks at rock bottom prices," she bragged about her savvy investment skills.

"Good, I can't retire soon enough." He shook his head with frustration. He'd obviously had a long day at work.

Leila went back to the television. Lilly Allen Garrison, a WAOK News commentator said, "The media nicknamed the virus which depletes the body's zinc supply and severely weakens the immune system. One of the symptoms of zinc evaporating from the body is an extreme metallic body odor. They're now calling 61-DIVOC—the Big Zinc Stink."

Chapter Six

49 days after first human dies of 61-DIVOC

"She added a pinch of arsenic to the tax man's tea, just to be sure." Leila finished her author reading with thunderous applause. She and her mother represented two of the lucky six local authors invited to read an excerpt from their books at the Jacksonville Book Fest. Hundreds of local authors sat at tables to sell and sign their books to the masses at the Downtown Jacksonville Public Library.

"Thank you for reading to us today," Janine, a Book Fest Volunteer, shook Leila's hand.

"Thanks for having us." Leila studied the book shelves and found all thirteen of her books on display. "Mom, look."

"Oh, wow. But where are my books?" Mom asked.

"They're probably all checked out." Leila tapped briskly on her iPhone, opened the Jacksonville Public Library app and typed in her mother's name. "Yep, someone checked out all of your books."

"Huh, well, let's go sell some more books." Mom slowly walked from the podium back to their table. Since Mom couldn't walk very far, the Book Fest coordinator hooked them up with a premium table close to the library's entrance which provided tons of foot traffic.

"I can't believe how many books we sold today. That's a record for both of us," Leila said with a pleasantly surprised tone.

"But you've sold a lot more than me." Mom sat down at the table.

Leila sat in the chair next to her mother and prepared to rake in the dough. "Since so many readers bought my Cauldron Series books today, I changed my reading selection at the last minute," Leila referred to her books about witches.

"Which story did you plan to read initially?" Mom asked.

"*Zinc,* one of the short stories in my *Elements of Mystery Collection.*" Leila referred to her recently published short story collection which contained 118 stories, each titled after all 118 named elements in the Periodic Table.

"What's *Zinc* about again?" Mom asked.

"*Zinc's* premise is the true story about a shark chasing Damon while he surfed at Playalinda Beach. Luckily, Damon caught a wave and rode safely to shore. To tie the element to the story, Damon applied zinc oxide on his face to avoid sunburn," Leila said.

"Oh, yeah. I had no idea that really happened to Damon until I read *Zinc.*" Mom shivered at the horrific notion of a shark chasing her only son. "What are Luke and the boys doing today?" Mom asked.

Leila rolled her eyes. "Building a desalination contraption," Leila said, matter-of-factly, like building a desalinator is a normal, everyday occurrence.

"A what?" Mom asked.

"Desalination removes the salt from salt water. The Saint John's River is fresh water. But since we're only 8 miles from the Atlantic Ocean, the river water from our dock is brackish."

"I know the definition of desalination," Mom said with a condescending tone. "But why do you need that?"

"If Armageddon starts and we no longer have running water, we won't die of dehydration," Leila explained.

"Is Luke really this scared about the virus?" Mom asked with her worry wort tone.

"Oh, yeah. But it gets worse. He bought giant rain barrels and diversion gutters to collect rain water," Leila said.

Mom arched her eyebrows. "Wow, he's gone off the deep end."

"Oh, it gets even worse," Leila said with an annoyed tone.

"Worse?"

"He bought tons of tablets to kill bacteria in the ground water and enough filters to processes one million gallons of water."

"Is that what's in all of those five-gallon buckets in the guest bedroom?" Mom asked.

"No, those buckets are filled with bags of rice and dried beans. We have enough food to last at least 4 months," Leila said.

"Does he really think it'll get that bad? I heard on the news that President Ace placed a 'Do Not Travel Ban' on flights coming in from China, Korea, Iran and Italy," Mom said.

Leila shrugged. "Hopefully he's overreacting. The media thought so and blasted President Ace for the travel ban. They called him racist and xenophobic."

At least no one has died in the United States yet

Bzzzzzz

Leila's iPhone buzzed

WAOK News Alert
First Death in the United States from 61-DIVOC Virus

"Oh shit!" Leila said with an alarming tone.

"What?" Mom asked.

"The first death in the United States from the Zink Stink virus." Leila grimaced.

"Oh, dear. Hopefully a Floridian didn't die," Mom said.

"Hold on. I'll read the article." Leila scrolled through her iPhone and read the news out loud, "Washington State. That's about as far away as you can get from Florida within the Continental United States. It says that the man who died tested positive for the virus after returning from a trip to Wuhoo, China where he visited family over the holidays."

Chapter Seven

61 days after first human dies of 61-DIVOC

The Logan Family arrived at TPC—The Player's Championship. Their corporate tent passes didn't start until 2 p.m. which gave them time to walk around.

"Oh, they moved the mock tee to the front entrance." Leila referred to a miniature version of the famous 17th Hole where the green occupied a tiny island in the middle of the pond.

"Hey, Mom. We'll be in here." Zach and David scurried off to get in line to challenge their golf skills.

"Okay. We'll be there in a minute. We need beer." Leila led Luke to the nearest beer tent. After sampling a few locally crafted beers, Leila ordered a hoppy IPA and Luke ordered a dark beer.

"Cheers," they said in unison as they tapped their plastic cups. A cold beer on an unusually hot day in March hits the spot.

"Did I hear correctly that this is the last day TPC is open to the public?" Leila asked before taking another generous sip of beer.

"Yes, players only on Friday, Saturday and Sunday," Luke said and grabbed her hand as they strolled back towards the mini 17th Hole.

"Good thing I'm not important enough at work to score Friday, Saturday or Sunday tent passes. I'm only important enough for Thursday's round."

"It's too bad your parents couldn't be here," Luke referred to Leila's father and daughter tradition of attending the golf tournament almost every year since 1996. Mom started tagging along a few years ago when she grew addicted to watching golf. Her mother's last-minute minor surgery yesterday kept her parents from attending this year.

Leila and Luke joined the boys who now stood in front of the line. Luke opted out and stood on the sidelines to take pictures and videos of her and the boys. When Leila's turn arrived, she said to Luke with an exaggerated Southern Accent, "'Here, hold my beer.'" She laughed at the famous quote that guys said to one another before attempting something stupid.

Leila instinctively reached for the club, but then hesitated. *Do I really want to touch this club that someone else just used?* Using precaution, she doused her hands with hand sanitizer. The easily spread virus forced everyone to frequently wash their hands and use hand sanitizer.

"Mom, Zach made it to the island without hitting the ball into the water." David pointed.

"Good job, Son." Leila teed her ball, swung and missed.

"Wow, Mom. You really suck," Zach said.

"'That's what she said,'" she quoted the famous line from the hit television series—*The Office.*

"Ew, Mom." Zach rolled his eyes like an annoyed teenager.

Leila's second swing struck the ball, but it only flew a few feet. *Plunk.* Her next two balls splashed into the water, too.

"Don't quit your day job." Luke laughed.

"Don't put that on Facebook." Leila quipped and doused her hands again with homemade hand sanitizer.

"Mom, we're meeting some friends. We'll see you at the tent at 2." The boys waved as they walked away to meet their friends.

"Okay. Remember the tent is in a different spot. It's on the 16th Fairway with a great view of the 16th and 17th Greens." Leila retrieved her beer from Luke and asked, "Do you want to watch some golf?"

"At a golf tournament?" Luke laughed at his own joke.

Leila studied the line up to see which golfers played through the course when and where. "Anyone you want to see?"

"What's his face," Luke referred to his favorite golfer who drew the biggest crowds.

"Nope, he teed off early this morning. Mom wants a picture of Prince," she referred to her mom's favorite golfer. Ire still filled her every time she saw Prince because he got beaucoup bucks to wear their company logo on his hat. But then the company grew stingy with its employees' annual raises.

"Prince comes through 16 soon, same with that hot Irish dude. Let's get another beer and find a nice spot in the shade. Then we'll be right by the tent when it opens in an hour," Luke said.

"Twist my arm." They walked to the beer tent and repeated their previous order. As they walked to the 16th Green, Leila noticed people in the bank's tent. "Huh? The invite says 2 to 4, but there are people in the tent."

"I thought they hosted another event in the morning, then closed down from 1 to 2 to clean and replenish the food," he said.

"I wonder what's happening?"

Bzzzzz

Bzzzzz

Their iPhones buzzed simultaneously. Leila stared at the WAOK News Alert.

The Players Championship cancelled the rounds on Friday, Saturday and Sunday

Sink The Zinc

Chapter Eight

61 days after first human dies of 61-DIVOC

"Damn, we could've saved twenty bucks if we'd known that the tent opened early." Leila walked up to one of the tent volunteers and asked, "Our passes say 2, but are we allowed in early?"

"Sure. Once we heard that they cancelled the rest of the tournament, we decided to let everyone stay. In fact, we're not closing until today's round finishes. We've got lots of food and alcohol that the bank already paid for," the volunteer wearing a light-blue golf shirt and beige slacks said.

Leila mentally applauded her company's wise decision to change the color of the volunteers' wardrobe. In the past, they wore red shirts with beige pants to match the colors of the bank's logo. Leila always joked that people would think they worked at Target instead of the bank.

"Cool. Thank you. Our sons are coming later, but they have their passes," Leila said.

The volunteer checked them in, affixed paper bands to their wrists and said, "Have a great afternoon."

Cold air conditioning greeted them. "Oh, that feels good." Leila moaned. They quickly found a table up front with a great view of the 17th Green and a giant flat-screen. Leila placed her beer on the table and grabbed two bottles of cold water from the bar.

"Text the boys and let them know that the tent opened early." Luke chugged half the water in one big gulp.

Leila texted the boys, and a picture popped up on her iPhone. "Ah, it's my cousin, Erin. She and her family are at Disney for the next few days. You've met them before the last time they visited from Missouri. We met them at Animal Kingdom."

"Oh, yeah. They have twins, right?" Luke finished his water.

"Wow, good memory. Ah, man," Leila said.

"What?" Luke asked.

"They're on the new Star Wars ride—Rise of the Resistance." Although happy for her cousin and her family, Leila grew a tad jealous that they got to ride the new Star Wars ride at Hollywood Studios before her.

"Did I ride that?" Luke took a big sip of beer.

"No, even I haven't ridden it. You need to arrive at Hollywood Studios before they open at 7 a.m. Once you're in the park, you log onto the Disney app and join a virtual queue which fills up within minutes. Then they give you a boarding time which could be as late as 9 p.m. when the park closes." Leila sipped her beer.

"Guess I'll never ride that." Luke finished his beer.

"And even if you get a boarding pass, you're not guaranteed to ride it because it keeps breaking down. I've heard that people waited in the real line for hours and still didn't get to ride it," she said.

Luke pushed his empty beer cup towards her. His subtle hint for her to procure more booze.

"Would you like another drink?" she asked.

"Sure."

"Would you like me to get it?" she asked.

"Sure," Luke said, planted to his seat with his eyes glued to the flat-screen.

Leila decided on Bloody Marys, especially since their sons drove them. One of the perks of having teenaged drivers. Leila wisely decided to add her own olives and limes to their drinks to avoid cooties from the bartender. This *new normal* seemed rather odd.

The boys walked in, joined them at their table and asked, "Where's the food?"

Starving teenage boys. "I overhead someone say soon. Remember, the ticket says 2," Leila said.

"What's in the bags?" Luke asked.

"We scored all kinds of free stuff." The boys proudly displayed their loot of golf paraphernalia.

Leila scrolled through Facebook and viewed all of her cousin's pictures at Disney. "I can't believe that they risked getting the virus. Disney's a giant cesspool for germs. You know, David, you and I should've been at Disney earlier this week."

"No, shit," David said.

Leila had planned three days with David at Disney. She'd looked forward to spending quality time with her firstborn during his Spring Break. But she grew uber paranoid about this virus and would never forgive herself if he caught it because she took him to Disney. Not only did she cancel this week's trip, she also cancelled next week's trip with her nieces during their Spring Break.

"Finally! Food!" an obviously starving Zach said.

Leila's received another text from her cousin with a picture from the new Mickey and Minnie's Runaway Railway that recently opened up where the Great Movie Ride used to be.

She texted back—*So jealous, but happy for ya'll.*

Erin texted back, and the message shocked her.

"Holy shit!" Leila said.

"What?" Luke asked.

"Remember Valentine's day three years ago when we ate at Le Cellier in EPCOT?" Leila asked.

"Yes, I still can't believe that you finessed our way into one of the most popular restaurants at Disney on Valentine's Day without a reservation," he said.

"Remember when I said, 'We'll know the world will end when Disney closes?'"

"Yep."

Still staring at her phone incredulously, she said, "My cousin just heard shocking news from one of the Cast Members—Disney closes March 16, 2020!"

Chapter Nine

62 days after first human dies of 61-DIVOC

"Welcome to Moe's," an employee said as Leila and David entered one of David's favorite restaurants.

They ordered their food, filled their drink cups with sweet tea and quickly found a booth.

"Great movie," Leila referred to the movie she and her oldest son just saw at AMC—*Jumanji: The Next Level*. She savored this one-on-one time with her movie buddy on the last day of his Spring Break.

"Yeah, I really enjoyed it." David sipped his sweet tea as he studied his iPhone. "Oh shit."

"What?" Leila asked.

"Guess you're stuck with me for two more weeks. UCF closed to stop the spread."

"Of Socialism?" Leila jokingly referred to the annoying Liberal views of colleges and universities.

"Good one, Mom," David said.

"I'm not surprised. Florida's Governor closed all public schools for the next two weeks." Leila sipped sweet tea as a Moe's employee delivered their food to the table.

"Zach has the next two weeks off, too?" David asked.

"Presumably. Bishop Kenny usually follows Duval County Public Schools regarding closures, like they do with hurricanes. But with the Schoology program, I'm sure he'll just do his classwork on his iPad in his room." Leila took a big bite of her chicken quesadilla cleverly named—Don't Talk about Chicken Club.

"Our exchange students from Italy said they cancelled school for the rest of the year." David bit into his Wrong Doug stack.

"With all the death in Italy, especially the elderly, why would New York wait so long to close the schools? Florida's Governor announced closing schools before New York's Governor did. The closures all start next week, but New York's virus cases started weeks before Florida's." Leila dunked a tortilla chip into cheese queso.

"Stupid Blue State," David referred to the nickname of a Democrat-run state.

Leila rolled her eyes. "Don't get me started. I can't believe New York's Governor sent 61-DIVOC survivors back into nursing homes. He should've quarantined them somewhere. President Ace even sent the giant Naval hospital ship, *the USNS Comfort,* to New York Harbor just to accommodate all the cases. New York barely used the ship and thousands of senior citizens died in nursing homes because of the Governor's incompetence and stupidity."

"Is Great-Aunt Judy okay?" David asked.

"Yeah, she's fine. Luckily her assisted living facility in Titusville stopped allowing visitors a while back, but reported zero cases. Poor Judy has no idea what's happening in the world."

"Did you hear Hank Thomas has the Zinc Stink?" David asked.

"Yes. Poor guy is stuck in another country," Leila said.

"Uh, Hank Thomas is definitely *not* poor."

"Ooh, I just thought of another conspiracy theory. Governor Cumwad of New York wants all of the old people to die because New York assesses a separate Estate Tax."

"What's an Estate Tax?" David asked.

"When you die with a lot of money, the IRS and most states tax the crap out if it. New York has a gazillion millionaires, even billionaires," Leila explained.

"Wow! Murdering old people to collect more taxes, that's a stretch of the imagination. Even for you, Mom," David said.

Leila shrugged. "Occupational hazard."

"Have you heard about all the Jerry Hapstein conspiracy theories?" David asked.

"Not really, but I heard he didn't really commit suicide. Someone murdered him in his jail cell even with security guards and cameras. Supposedly some famous people didn't want Hapstein testifying about who visited his pedophile island of child sex slaves." Leila cringed at the horrid acts of some of the rich and famous.

"Google it when you get home. But sadly, human trafficking runs rampant throughout the world," David said.

"I will. One good thing about closing all the schools. Jerry Hapstein's pedophile, child sex ring can't abduct any more kids if they're safe at home."

Chapter Ten

70 days after first human dies of 61-DIVOC

"I'm going for my walk. Good luck installing those hurricane shutters," Leila said to Luke and the boys. She loved her daily walks outside, weather permitting of course. She walked five miles in her neighborhood while lifting weights and watching Disney Plus on her iPhone. She also chit chatted with her neighbors and enjoyed the beautiful view of the Saint John's River and abundant birds in the marsh and preserve.

"Hi, Leila." Her next-door neighbor, Hamid, walked his dog, Safid.

"Hey, Safid." Leila immediately petted the white border collie.

"What are Luke and the boys doing?" he asked while gesturing to them schlepping the hurricane shutters to the back of the house.

"Installing hurricane shutters." She didn't want to tell him that these hurricane shutters served a double purpose—hurricanes and a barricade to protect them from looters during Armageddon.

"Why put them up now? You're not going to keep them up until October, are you?" His tone implied his concern for the neighborhood's appearance.

"No, just a test install including drilling all of the holes for the bases to make sure that they fit. Makes it easier to hang for the next hurricane. Hurricanes Matthew and Irma scared the crap out of us."

"Us, too. Enjoy your walk," he said.

Leila petted Safid one last time, then opened the Disney Plus app and hit the resume button. After getting Disney Plus as a Christmas present, she first watched *Mandalorian* with baby Yoda. Then she rewatched all of the *Star Wars* movies in chronological order. Now she enjoyed all of the Disney animated classics in the order of their original release in the theaters.

A WAOK News alert appeared on her phone.

Italy's one day death toll reaches 80
New Jersey issues stay-at-home order

What? Why didn't New Jersey impose stay-at-home orders before now? Stupid Blue Sate.

She arrived at the end of the street and her nearly eighty-year-old neighbor, Dr. Duane, greeted her. "Hi, Leila. I'm ready for another book from you and your mom. I really enjoyed reading *Carbon Copy* and *Make Old Bones.*"

"Thank you. I'll bring you the next books in each of our series on my next lap." Leila walked away and turned around at the entrance to the neighborhood. Even though they lived in a nice, gated community, bad areas existed just beyond the gate.

Her neighbor, Melinda, Hamid's wife, drove up to the gate in her new, red Tesla. She rolled down the window and smiled. "Hi, Leila. How are you? We need to get together with the girls and drink wine." She referred to their occasional get togethers with some of the ladies in the neighborhood. They'd coined themselves—The Real Housewives of St. John's Cay.

"I'm thrilled that the IRS extended the tax deadline until July 15th. I'm normally working my ass off this time of year. But instead, I'm outside enjoying this beautiful weather" She gestured to the gorgeous sky above. "How are ya'll?" Leila asked.

"We're good, but working from home presents challenges, especially with crappy Comcast. And sometimes we drive each other nuts." Melinda rolled her eyes.

"We have tickets to see *Hamilton* tomorrow, but I'm glad they rescheduled. We've had several concerts postponed, too—REO Speedwagon, Psychedelic Furs, Elton John, Journey, Green Day, Roger Waters of Pink Floyd and the big stadium tour with Def Leppard, Mötley Crüe, Poison and Joan Jett. I *hate* this pandemic, but it's nice having David home from UCF," Leila said. She referred to closures for the rest of the school year.

"I know. It's so scary. I'm terrified to leave the house. And what's with this toilet paper shortage. Who saw that coming?" Melinda asked.

Leila remained silent about their hoard of toilet paper because Luke predicted this whole mess. "Oh, I know. And what's with all of these cruise ships?" Leila gestured to the four cruise ships visible from their neighborhood.

"No one wants to take a cruise these days. I guess they gotta park them somewhere because there are more ships than berths," Melinda said.

"Something seems suspicious. I think that something else is really happening and this virus is merely a distraction," Leila said with an ominous tone and a shiver.

"You know, I bet your right. There is definitely more going on than what they're telling us." Melinda grimaced at the horrible notion.

"I should write a book about a pandemic distracting everyone from one of my conspiracy theories," Leila laughed.

Melinda laughed, too. "Great talking to ya. Ya'll stay safe." Melinda waved as the Tesla window rolled up.

"You, too. Have a great day." Leila waved. As she resumed her walk, dozens of story ideas swam in her head. She walked one more lap, dropped off *Tin Roof* and *Bred in the Bone* at the good doctor's front door and collected twenty bucks. As she walked back home, her imagination ran wild. This much inspiration didn't often flood her brain. She gave up on her five-mile goal and went home to jot down all of her ideas for her new book.

Chapter Eleven

74 days after first human dies of 61-DIVOC

Leila shot up in bed and gasped for air. Panic rose in her chest. *Did she contract 61-DIVOC?* She wrapped her arms around herself to calm down. She breathed deep and slow, hoping to mitigate a potential panic attack, but still gasped for air. Her heart raced, her hands and feet tingled, and the blood flowing through her veins felt like fire. She coughed several times and spat a nasty loogie into a tissue. Coughing, fever and shortness of breath. She'd heard about these symptoms. She climbed out of bed and checked her temperature. The thermometer beeped, and relief washed through her when it read 97.6.

Unsure what to do, she jumped into the shower. *If I need to go to the hospital, I'd better shower and do my hair first.* Her mom would've rationalized that if she worried about her hair, then she'd be okay.

Luke walked into the bathroom just as she stepped out of the shower. "Woohoo! You're naked. But what are you doing up so early?" he referred to her normally not getting out of bed until 8 a.m.

"Luke, I feel like crap. I'm coughing and I feel like I'm not breathing in enough oxygen." Fear filled her as she said the words out loud.

"Did you catch the Zink Stink?" he asked jovially.

"I'm serious. I think I should go to the Emergency Room." She dried off, lathered Nivea lotion all over her body and donned her white, plush Disney robe.

Luke grimaced. "Oh, God. Don't go to the Emergency Room, then you'll definitely get the virus. Go to urgent care. It's probably just bronchitis. You get it every winter."

"That's true. But if I get bronchitis while I have the virus, I may never recover." Her hands shook as fear ripped through her.

He smelled her and shrugged. "You don't stink. But then again, you just got out of the shower."

"I'll go to urgent care. At least they can treat me for bronchitis," she rationalized.

"Keep me posted." He kissed her.

She arrived at Care Spot, put on a mask and checked in. The lady scanned her credit card and handed it back with her bare hands. *I can't believe she's touching something that I just touched with her bare hands.* Leila took the credit card, wiped it down with a Clorox wipe, then doused her hands with sanitizer. A nurse escorted her to a room right away.

Leila sat on the examination table, and the doctor walked in wearing a face shield, hazmat scrubs and gloves. Even with all of that protective gear, she still stood six feet away.

"What brings you in?" the doctor asked.

"I'm coughing up nasty stuff and having trouble breathing." Leila took a deep and labored breath.

The doctor took her temperature—still normal. Then she obviously felt safe enough to examine her. "Take deep breaths." She listened to her lungs, took her blood pressure and said, "You have high blood pressure and your hands are shaking. I think you're having a panic attack and you have bronchitis. I'll prescribe an inhaler, an antibiotic and a steroid to clear your lungs."

"You don't think I have the virus?" Leila asked.

"No. Your oxygen levels are perfect. But you can go to the Jaguar stadium and get tested for the virus," the doctor said.

"Thank you, doctor."

Leila exited Care Spot, hopped into her Gator-blue pathfinder, drove towards the stadium and called Luke.

"You gonna live?" he asked.

"Yep. The doctor doesn't think I have the virus. She's treating me for bronchitis and thinks I'm having a panic attack. But I'm headed to the stadium to get tested."

"Why would you do that?" His tone rang with ire.

"To see if I have the virus," Leila said, not sure why this angered him.

"Why? There's nothing they can do even if you have the virus. And if you do have it, then I can't work and I'm screwed. Just stay home and quarantine yourself," he said.

"Oh, okay. I didn't think of it that way. Can you please pick up my prescriptions from Publix on your way home from work so I don't spread my cooties around?" she asked.

"Sure. There is something fishy about all of this testing. They're marking people. I heard that if you test positive, they track your phone. And if you go out anywhere, big brother notifies all of the phones around you that you have the virus," he said with an ominous tone.

"That's a scary thought. They say, 'Big Brother is always watching.' See ya at home."

"Bye."

"Bye."

Leila contemplated Luke's words. "There's definitely something fishy about all of this testing. They're marking people." *What if everyone who tests positive gets rounded up and quarantined on a cruise ship to stop the spread. What if they decide to give up on the positive cases and let the infected humans die on the ships?*

Sink The Zinc

Chapter Twelve

81 days after first human dies of 61-DIVOC

"Are you coming?" Luke hollered from the hot tub on the patio.

"Chill, Luke! Just watching news highlights." Leila stood in front of the television watching the local news wearing her Gator-blue bikini and flip flops.

> *Safer at home orders start at midnight for the entire state of Florida*
> *Worldwide cases of 61-DIVOC reach one million*
> *Four people died of the virus in Jacksonville today*
> *The city's total death toll is 9 with 286 total cases*
> *Most cases and deaths are from nursing homes*
> *Only 7% of Jacksonville's 61—DIVOC tests came back positive.*

"Leila, our wine won't pour itself," Luke hollered.

He's got a point there. Leila turned off the news, opened a big bottle of cabernet sauvignon and grabbed Luke's stainless-steel sippy cup and her stainless-steel wine goblet. *Wouldn't want to break a wine glass in the new hot tub.*

She set down hers and Luke's wine on their respective cup holders and climbed into the hot tub. *Ahhhhh!* They'd just bought the hot tub in early March after filling in their pool, removing the rusty screened enclosure and installing 1700 square feet of pavers. Buying a hot tub in late February and early march offered the best deals because the pool and spa stores needed to make room for the new spring stuff. Since they bought the hot tub a month ago, they'd spent every evening drinking wine in the hot tub.

"Cheers." Leila clinked Luke's sippy cup and gulped a generous amount.

"I noticed you stocked up on Armageddon supplies, too," Luke referred to the dozens of red wine bottles she'd procured over the last few weeks.

"Publix thinks I'm an alcoholic, by the way. I'm obviously not hosting a party. I thought myself clever buying 4 bottles in one wine bag, taking them to the car, then going back in to buy 4 more at a different cash register. Damn bag girl busted me. She asked, 'Back again?'"

"'Dope,'" Luke said Homer Simpson's famous line.

"Winn Dixie doesn't judge, by the way," she said.

"Good to know. I received my official letter from the United Launch Alliance certifying me as an essential employee for our nation's defense." He sipped wine.

"Good, you can go to work tomorrow and pay for all of this." Leila gestured at their beautiful new patio.

"If I get pulled over driving to Cape Canaveral, I show them my letter and go to work," he said.

"Do you really think they'll randomly pull people over for not staying home?" she asked.

"I hope not." He finished his wine.

"Cruise ship." Another Norwegian cruise ship floated by in their back yard. Three Norwegian ships rotated between their backyard and downtown Jacksonville. "There's something suspicious with these cruise ships. Like today, Fort Lauderdale allowed a Holland America ship to dock there because Europe didn't want all those cooties. Florida gladly accepted the ship, quarantined its sick passengers and flew the healthy ones back to Europe. Now America has another empty cruise ship."

"You and your conspiracy theories. Any alien invasion theories?" he asked jovially.

"I'm glad you asked. But you'll want a refill for this one." Leila left the soothing comfort of the jets to lean out of the hot tub and pour more wine. She'd conveniently left the open bottle on the top step to avoid getting chilled from the breeze. She refilled their wine, handed Luke his cup and took an enormous sip. "Drink up," she said.

Luke obeyed.

"My conjuring mind terrifies you enough to not read my stories," she said and sipped wine.

"Give me a little credit. I've read some of your stories. But now you've got me worried." He gulped wine.

"Remember when you told me *not* to get a 61-DIVOC test because they'd mark me? I feared they'd round up all of the positive cases, put them on a cruise ship and sink it," she said.

"I remember telling you not to take the test, but you never shared that theory with me. But what's that got to do with an alien invasion?" he asked.

"What if the aliens are behind the whole virus as a way to get people to take tests to see if they've lost their immune system. What if aliens plan to take over the Human Race and they need humans as hosts for breeding? They don't want humans who have the Zinc Stink; they want human hosts with healthy immune systems. Or they're trying to create an alien-human hybrid by mating with healthy humans."

Luke's face grew pale. He stared at the Dames Point Bridge and remained silent. Dozens of military jets and helicopters flew overhead towards the bridge.

Worry rushed through Leila. "You think I'm bat shit crazy, don't you? More wine?" she asked.

"Is it me or is the moon rising much quicker than normal?" he asked.

Leila studied the moon like they did every night. The moon definitely looked different, much bigger than normal. She knew because she'd studied it every night for the last month. "It *is* moving faster than normal. And there's some weird knob at the end."

"Yeah. I don't know what the fuck that is or why all those jets and helicopters are flying towards it."

"So, I'm not bat shit crazy?" she asked.

"I hope you are." He grimaced.

She studied the rising moon and said, "Maybe we've had too much to drink. But the moon resembles a UFO!"

Chapter Thirteen

89 days after first human dies of 61-DIVOC

I need to stop watching the news! Leila told herself as she turned off the television. It saddened her to think that the Zinc Stink killed so many people. President Ace and the Surgeon General accurately warned them that this would be the worst week for Americans. Unfortunately, the United States suffered more deaths than any other country—nearly twenty thousand. Today marked the highest one-day death toll worldwide—twenty-two hundred. That's assuming China reported their numbers correctly. Conspiracy theorists speculated that China lied about everything from the very beginning, especially the severity of the virus.

Rumors speculated that corrupt Communist China and the World Health Organization acted in cahoots. The Vice President threatened to stop funding the WHO altogether. Luckily, President Ace vowed to move more manufacturing jobs away from China and back to America, especially the manufacturing and pharmaceutical industries.

At least some good news broadcasted this week— that socialist sack of shit dropped out of the running for the Democratic presidential nominee. The sole Democratic survivor—Beaux Jaden—proved the lesser of two evils. Infamously handsy with the ladies, many speculated that it was only a matter of time before a former intern spoke up about her *Me Too* moment with the Presidential candidate.

Leila vowed not to watch the news any more today. She carried her laptop to the sunroom and enjoyed the beautiful view of the Saint Johns River. Bald Eagles flew out of the preserve and towards her house.

The beauty of America's mascot flying majestically and freely filled her with American Pride.

Geese floated in the pond. "Babies!" The new batch of goslings thrilled her. The mom, dad and goslings walked up onto the shore. After counting seven baby Ryans, she mentally patted herself on the back for her clever reference to one of her favorite actors—Ryan Gosling.

The family of geese walked along the shoreline and towards her patio. *Oh, no! Please don't come onto our patio.* Leila feared her own indoor/outdoor cats would harm the baby Ryans. All three of her kitties had previously caught birds and brought them into the house, sometimes still alive. *Yikes!* She also feared that if one of the cats pounced on a gosling, the protective geese parents might harm her precious kitties. Given the beautiful spring weather, she'd left the doors to the patio open so the cats could go in and out of the house as they pleased.

When the geese and goslings got close to the patio, Leila opened the window, clapped her hands loudly and hollered at the geese, "Get out of here!" Luckily, that startled the geese, and they scurried into the preserve. *Phew!*

Leila opened her laptop and said, "Now, where was I?" She referred to writing her latest book. And big surprise, it contained a virus and a dozen conspiracy theories. But in her book, she literally wrote her own happy ending. Writing this book helped her cope with this virus and all the death. It also provided a much-needed distraction.

For weeks now, she'd convinced herself that the government faked a pandemic to distract the world from something much bigger—the end of the world. She contemplated the rising cases and deaths worldwide, and an epiphany struck. *How do we know the pandemic statistics are even real? Who counts those? For all we know, it's just numbers on a television screen. What if it's just another example of Fake News?*

Fortunately, Leila personally neither knew of anyone who died from 61-DIVOC, nor anyone who even tested positive for the virus. Then her mind continued on the same thread. Not only did she not know anyone who caught the Zinc Stink, she didn't know anyone who *knew* of anyone with the virus. Albeit, a few celebrities tested positive, like Hank Thomas. *But with the overabundance of Fake News, who can really know these celebrities actually contracted and recovered from 61-DIVOC?*

Then Leila's mind really spiraled downward. She recalled a scene from a movie. In the movie, the government placed a giant dome over a city which trapped all of its citizens away from the rest of the world. But the city filmed a commercial starring Hank Thomas as a spokesperson in favor of the dome. *Who wouldn't trust such a beloved actor?* Leila theorized that the Fake News media convinced the actor to tell the world that he contracted and subsequently recovered from the fake virus to fool the world to believe the virus existed.

As Leila corralled her overactive imagination, something squealed downstairs. *What the hell?* She'd feared the worse—a cat caught one of the baby Ryans and brought it into the house. Not wanting to face a dying gosling, she hollered, "Boys, quick, go downstairs. I think one of the cats brought in another critter!"

David ran out of his room and descended the stairs in record time. "Oh, my, God! Mom, I think it's a bunny! Sabbath cornered it, but I'm putting the cat outside. It's okay to come down."

Leila headed downstairs, relieved for the unharmed bunny. Small enough to hold in the palm of your hand, the bunny hid in a corner behind the legs of a side table. "Quick! Get the other cats out of here and find something to put the bunny in."

David obeyed. But one of the cats spotted the bunny and approached curiously. The bunny hopped across the foyer and tried to jump onto the lowest step of the staircase, but his legs proved too tiny hop up. David swooped in, picked up the bunny and placed him in an empty Amazon cardboard box. The bunny scurried around in the box, then tried to hide in the corner.

"He looks unharmed, and there's no blood. As fast as he hopped, he's probably fine." Leila studied the terrified bunny adoringly.

"It looks like a bunny, but his ears and feet are really small," David said.

"It's a marsh rabbit, like the ones we see at Disney. They don't get very big." Leila admired the adorable bunny.

David reached in, picked it up and held the bunny protectively with both hands. "Mom, he's shivering."

"Ah, poor little fellow. He's terrified." Leila petted the top of the bunny's head.

"Can I keep him?" David asked. "My college apartment is pet friendly."

"Go dig that old fish tank out of the garage. Marsh rabbits eat aquatic vegetation. Put some reeds, grass and watercress from the marsh into the tank. But you're cleaning his cage and feeding him. Rabbits poop *a lot*," Leila ordered.

Her heart warmed watching her grown son fall in love with a bunny. With Easter Sunday only two days away, today proved a truly Good Friday after all. And for the first time since the Zinc Stink started, Leila felt an overwhelming sense of hope.

Chapter Fourteen

99 days after first human dies of 61-DIVOC

Leila walked outside to find Luke hooking up their new rain barrels to a diverted downspout from their rain gutters. "Well, Jacksonville just made WAOK News because we reopened our beaches with restrictions."

"Did your mom tell you that?" Luke laughed at his own joke because Leila's mother *loathed* WAOK News.

"Good one. Oh, I started buying back into the Stock Market today because stocks are cheap these days. I wish I would've started buying back last week when the Dow dipped into the teens."

"Are we ready to retire?" Luke wiped the sweat from his brow and walked inside.

She followed him inside. "Not yet. But I sold VTI back in February at $170/share and bought it back today at $130."

"Sweet. I'm buying two more rain barrels." Luke walked into the kitchen and poured himself a glass of ice water.

"Did you hear about this?" Leila turned up the volume of WAOK News. It showed a video clip where Kathy Kunt bragged about her gourmet cupcakes in front of her Sub-Zero refrigerator and freezer combo while homeless people in her district starved in the streets.

Luke quickly drank water and poured himself another glass. "Yes. That bitch has my dream refrigerator and freezer."

"That's not the point," Leila said.

"I know. Just saying. But her bony old ass should be back in Washington getting the next phase of the stimulus package approved. She blocked it by putting all of her stupid and unnecessary shit into the package." Luke rolled his eyes in frustration.

"The WAOK News commentator, Lilly Allen Garrison, made a great comparison. Maria Antoinette said, 'Let them eat cake.' And Kathy Kunt said, 'Let them eat cupcakes,'" Leila rehashed.

"That's hysterical. Oh, we're not getting the vaccine, by the way," Luke changed the subject.

"Oh, I agree. But probably not for the same reason as you," Leila said.

"They're developing the vaccine too quickly without enough trials. This whole thing is so stupid." Luke shook his head.

"You'll never guess my reasoning," Leila said sarcastically.

"Let me guess. Another conspiracy theory," Luke speculated.

"*Duh*. Another reason that I think this virus is fake is because they're trying to scare us all to death so we'll line up in droves to take this vaccine. But the vaccine is not really a vaccine at all." Sick of seeing Kathy Kunt's cupcake video, Leila turned off the news.

"What the hell is it then?" Luke asked.

"Scholars predict that if the exponential population growth doesn't halt, mankind will eventually exhaust all of our natural resources and wipeout the Human Race. Remember that movie *Dante* when Robert Langdon stopped the plague from releasing in Istanbul?"

"Oh, yeah. I remember. Extremists groups opposing overpopulation tried to start a plague to kill off millions of humans to stop overpopulation," Luke said.

"Well, in the book, which is always better, they didn't release a plague. Instead, they released a virus that made one-third of the population sterile to stop overpopulation," Leila gave a quick synopsis of Dan Brown's book.

"You think that 61-DIVOC sterilizes humans?" Luke asked.

"No. They want the virus to scare everyone enough to take the vaccine. But it's not really a vaccine to prevent 61-DIVOC. It's really a shot to sterilize half of the population!"

Chapter Fifteen

105 days after first human dies of 61-DIVOC

Leila sat in the sunroom in her favorite gold chair and knocked out another chapter of her latest book. She loved the beautiful spring weather and enjoyed the light breeze blowing through the open windows. But she knew this wonderful April weather would inevitably change to the brutal heat and humidity of summer.

Sabbath jumped onto the headrest on the back of her chair and meowed for attention. Leila gladly scratched his head and cooed, "Who's my sweet boy."

Pumpkin, who's black and white coloring resembled a tuxedo, waltzed into the sunroom to join the party. Sabbath, the dominant male, leapt from the top of the headrest and pounced on poor Pumpkin. After a few hisses, Sabbath chased Pumpkin out of the sunroom with scampering paws.

Mittens, a tabby cat with white paws and a white chest, rested on Leila's legs and opened her eyes with an annoyed expression to nonverbally complain about the disruption of her nap.

Feeling accomplished for writing three chapters today, Leila backed up her word document and mentally applauded herself for the brilliance of her latest chapters with clever forward pointers. Deciding to check in with social media, she scrolled through the news feed. A headline caught her eye.

The most hurricanes in one season predicted for 2020
Meteorologists predict so many named storms that they'll exhaust the English alphabet and have to

utilize the entire Greek Alphabet to name all the hurricanes.

Oh, great. More hurricanes in 2020. Just what we need. That reminded her of another conspiracy theory—terrorists generated hurricanes off the coast of Africa to destroy the United States. She even wrote a short story about it—*Holmium*—which she'd recently published as a part of her short story collection—*Elements Of Mystery.*

A chanting noise echoed from the river. It grew louder and louder, and Leila found its origin—the Dames Point Bridge. Thousands of people stood on the bridge and chanted, "Sink the Zink! Sink the Zink! Sink the Zink!"

What the fuck? Incredulity filled her as protesters shouted at the four cruise ships filled with 61-DIVOC patients.

Leila got up and turned on the television in her bedroom. Not limited to just Jacksonville, WAOK News covered many protests across the country. Apparently, massive synchronized protesters chanted "Sink the Zink," at every cruise terminal in the United States. The screen showed multiple cities on the East Coast including—New York City, Charleston, Savannah, Jacksonville, Cape Canaveral, Tampa, St. Petersburg, Miami and Key West. States on the West Coast included—Alaska, Washington, Oregon and California.

WAOK News commentator, Lilly Allen Garrison, said, "This is the largest protest in the history of the United States, even bigger than the Boston Tea Party and the Civil Rights Movement. Millions of healthy Americans demand action against the further spread of the Zink Stink.

Leila watched in horror as the four cruise ships filled with 61-DIVOC patients headed out to sea while uninfected Americans chanted, "Sink the Zink! Sink the Zink! Sink the Zink!"

Chapter Sixteen

113 days after first human dies of 61-DIVOC

Happy Star Wars Day! Leila arose after a good night's sleep, ready to start her day. Ever since she gave up caffeine to reduce her anxiety, she slept like a baby. Optimistic that the economy would reopen very soon, she couldn't wait to put this nasty pandemic behind her and resume a normal life.

She refilled her water glass and walked into the sunroom. Her morning routine started with waking up her mind. She opened her iPad and did her daily crossword puzzle. Next, she'd do a sudoku puzzle, followed by two lessons of German on the Duolingo app. Once she finished her puzzles, she'd walk five miles while lifting hand weights and watching Disney Plus on her iPhone. She loved walking outside, getting fresh air and watching all of the beautiful birds fly overhead.

Five bald Eagles flew out of the preserve and skimmed the water of the Saint Johns River to catch their breakfast. Now that the three babies grew up enough to fly, they accompanied their parents to catch food. Hopefully an eagle wouldn't pick up one of her kitties. *Yikes!* Leila shuddered at the horrific notion.

She heard a really loud jet engine and spotted a giant plane in the sky. *Holy Shit! That's the biggest plane she'd ever seen.* The way it turned, she figured it intended to land at NAS JAX, the Naval Air Station. The clear, blue sky offered great visibility. With her great far-sighted vision, she read the words on the plane—United States of America.

Leila ran out of the sunroom and hollered, "Boys, wake up. Come into the sunroom, quick. Luke, come here, you gotta see this!"

A shirtless Zach appeared in the sunroom wearing pajama bottoms. "What the hell? Why do you gotta be so freakin' loud and annoying in the morning?"

"What do you mean, 'in the morning?' Mom's loud and annoying any time of day." David shuffled in, picked up Sabbath and rocked him like a baby.

Luke joined them, still in his pajama bottoms and Florida Gator tee shirt. He held a coffee cup in his hand and wore a shocked expression on his face. "You're never gonna believe this."

"You're never gonna believe this! Look!" She gestured towards the giant plane.

"Noooo, freakin' way!" Zach stared awestruck.

"Holy Shit, Batman!" David said.

"Air Force One." Leila beamed with American Pride. Five bald Eagles flew in front of them while Air Force One flew above.

"I'm not surprised." Luke shrugged.

"Why aren't you surprised?" Leila asked.

"That's what I wanted to tell you. We won the contest!" Luke hollered with a shocked tone.

"Which contest?" Leila asked." You enter a gazillion contests every weekend."

"We won President Ace's contest!" Luke shouted excitedly.

Leila gasped; she'd forgotten all about the contest that Luke entered back in January.

"The Secret Service picks us up at noon. They gave us a very specific packing list. Giddy up." Luke cracked an imaginary whip.

"That's in three hours. I better hop in the shower. I wish they would've given us more notice." She mentally tallied all of the things she needed to do and pack in such a short period of time.

"That's how they roll for security purposes," Luke said and snapped his fingers.

"But wait, why aren't you surprised to see Air Force One?" she asked.

"Leila, really? Come on, you're killing me." Luke rolled his eyes.

"What? I don't get it. Why won't you just answer the question?" Miffed, she crossed her arms.

"Dad, she's a blonde *and* a woman," Zach said with a sarcastic tone.

Leila thought hard for a moment, then the wonderful realization sank in. "Are we...?"

Luke smiled and said with an excited tone, "We're flying down to Ace Cay on Air Force One with President Ace!"

Chapter Seventeen

113 days after first human dies of 61-DIVOC

"Bring your pets?" Leila read the packing list for their weekend trip to Ace Cay. "I understand formal attire because they'll probably host some fancy, schmancy, hoity, toity dinner, but our wedding album? Seriously?" She grabbed her gator-blue, full length formal dress that she'd bought two years ago for her boss's granddaughter's wedding. Then she grabbed the matching strappy heels.

"Boys, are ya'll packed yet?" Luke hollered.

"Uh, er, Mom? We don't have any formal attire," Zach said.

"Pack the prom tuxedo. You rented it before they postponed prom, then all the retail stores closed down before you could return it. It's perfect." Leila smiled at her handsome son. It saddened her that her youngest son missed out on so many milestones his Senior year of high school. Luckily, he and his girlfriend, Jane, attended his school's prom plus her school's prom together during their junior year.

"I only have the fancy black suit I bought for your brother's wedding. I forgot that I'd already had a black suit when I bought it. David can pack my extra one," Luke said.

"That'll work. Boys, once you finish packing, please put the kitties in their carriers," Leila said.

"That should be fun," David said sarcastically.

"Herding cats." Leila laughed. She reread the packing list and double checked everything—bathing suit, cocktail dress, leisure clothes, sundress, passports, driver's license, laptops, iPad, cell phone. Not that she planned on working at Ace Cay.

"All packed?" Luke asked.

"I think so, but I feel like I'm packing for a cruise, not a weekend at Ace Cay. Eight pairs of shoes for three days." Then a sense of foreboding fell over her.

"No one is cruising anytime soon." Luke waived to the river where empty cruise ships once floated.

"Luke, you were right about cruise ships. You've said for years that they're a huge cesspool for germs." Leila grimaced.

"Wait, did you just say I was right?" Luke asked excitedly.

"Don't get too excited, the Secret Service will be here any minute. How do I look?" Leila turned to Luke. She wore one of her many pretty dresses. The blue in the dress made her blue eyes stand out.

"Beautiful." He kissed her.

"Mom, what should we do with Flap Jack? He's grown so much since Easter and he shits everywhere. I can't leave him enough food for three days because he eats and poops so much." David asked.

Luke and Leila exchange knowing expressions.

"Maybe you should let him go. He'll thrive in the marsh, and the cats won't be here to try and eat him again," Leila said with a saddened tone.

"Ah, man. This is hard. But yeah, you're right, we should let him go," David said.

"Wow, did my teenage son just tell me that I was right?" Leila smirked.

"Don't let it go to your head, Mom," David chided.

"Boys, please bring everything downstairs. Then we'll all say goodbye to the poop machine," Luke referred to Flap Jack.

After lugging everything downstairs, the family stood in the kitchen and took turns holding and petting Flap Jack. Leila held the bunny and petted his soft fur. "Ah, I'll miss this little guy. Have a good life, meet a nice bunny and make lots of babies." Leila handed Flap Jack back to David.

David walked outside holding the bunny. He walked across the patio and down to the marsh. He kissed Flap Jack on his head, then gently placed the bunny on the ground. Flap Jack quickly hopped into the protective covering of the marsh. A tear dropped on David's cheek while he sniffled back a sob.

Ding Dong.

Luke opened the door to find two men wearing black suits, white shirts and sunglasses. Their presence dominated the doorway.

"Are you the Logan Family?" Secret Service Agent One asked.

"Yes, we're all packed and ready to go." Leila gestured for them to take their luggage.

First, I must collect your cell phones." Agent One held out his hand.

The Logan Family surrendered their cell phones.

Agent One grabbed the suit cases and loaded them into the black Lincoln Navigator.

Agent Two opened the door to a black limousine.

"Can the cats ride in the limo with us?" Leila asked. "They're terrified. We'll need to talk to them reassuringly."

"Yes," Agent Two said, then grabbed the pet carriers effortlessly.

Leila climbed in first, then slid down the black leather seat.

"Whoa, this is awesome," David said as he climbed in. Zach followed, then Luke.

Number Two placed the pet carriers into the limo.

The boys explored every nook and cranny of the interior. "Wow, there's a full bar in here. Mom, may I please have a beer?" David asked.

Leila turned to Luke for guidance.

Luke said, "Only if you make your mother and me a Bloody Mary."

Leila turned to her husband and said with an incredulous tone, "Wow, look at you day drinking."

The boys made two Bloody Mary's and handed them to their parents. Then they each grabbed a Corona beer and removed the bottle caps.

Leila proposed a toast, "To President Ace."

Everyone clinked glasses and said, "To President Ace."

As the limo pulled out of the driveway, Leila sipped the delicious Bloody Mary and let the alcohol seep in. She turned to study their beautiful home, relieved to finally get out of the house for the first time in nearly two months. *But why did she feel like she left her home for the last time?*

Chapter Eighteen

113 days after first human dies of 61-DIVOC

The thirty-minute limo ride went smoothly, except for Sabbath whining from his pet carrier. Leila had learned from previous trips to the vet, that only one cat did the crying—the dominant one. Mittens and Pumpkin just let Sabbath cry on their behalf.

They arrived at NAS JAX, and Air Force One dominated the tarmac. The blue and white 747 had a red stripe. The plane boasted an American Flag painted on its blue and white tail. UNITED STATES OF AMERICA painted in blue letters dominated the white side of the plane. The white underbelly of the plane boasted the presidential seal.

They exited the limo, walked up the stairs and boarded Air Force One. Agent One stowed their luggage in the cargo area, and Agent Two carried their kitties in the carriers.

"Is the President onboard?" Leila asked.

"Yes, we'll escort you to see him shortly after takeoff," Agent Two said. He escorted them to their plush leather seats.

"Wow, this is so cool!" Zach exclaimed. Not even a nonchalant teenager could dismiss the power and grandeur of flying on Air Force One. They buckled their seatbelts, and the plane taxied on the tarmac. The roar of the massive engines resonated throughout the cabin as the plane rose in the air.

After the plane leveled off, a flight attendant served them each a flute of champagne.

"What are we celebrating?" Leila asked.

"Flying on Air Force One." The flight attendant winked.

Leila barely took her first sip when Secret Service Agent Two said, "Come with me to meet the President."

The family of four gulped the rest of their champagne, unbuckled their seatbelts, rose out of their chairs and followed the agent. Walking down the long corridor, they passed several seating areas. They passed a conference room and several sofas. Jacksonville's mayor read the *Florida Times Union* on one of the sofas. "What's he doing here?"

Luke shrugged.

They arrived at a door bearing the presidential seal at the back of the plane. Agent Two opened the door and said, "Mr. President, this is the Logan Family, the contest winners."

President Alexander Ace rose behind his desk angled in front of the back corner. He wore a black suit with a white shirt and red tie. His suit's lapel boasted an American flag pin.

Do I bow? Leila thought.

"Welcome to Air Force One." The President held out his hand to shake.

Luke shook it immediately, then the boys did, too.

Leila hesitated. *Why are we shaking hands when social distancing forbade it?*

"Don't worry, it's fine," the President said, reassuringly.

"It's an honor to meet you, Mr. President. Thank you for having us." Leila's *Spidey senses* warped into overdrive.

"Congratulations on winning my contest. You tweeted a great photograph. Here, take a seat." The President gestured towards a seating area.

"Thank you," Leila said and sat down on a brown leather sofa.

"I enjoyed reading your new book about a fake pandemic and conspiracy theories. I'm looking forward to seeing how it ends," President Ace said.

Both honor and shock shot through her. *How in the hell did he read her unfinished and unpublished novel saved only on her laptop?*

"Oh, thank you," Leila said skeptically. "But how...?"

"Big brother is always watching." President Ace smiled. "I loved all of your crazy conspiracy theories. You mention all of them to keep the reader guessing which one will come true. But how did you know that the pandemic merely distracted the world from the real danger?"

Chapter Nineteen

113 days after first human dies of 61-DIVOC

"Wait, what? I was right?" Leila asked, stunned that she predicted something catastrophic.

Nodding, he said, "Yes, but how did you figure it out?"

"Once I saw all the empty cruise ships floating in my backyard, I grew suspicious. Plus, the numbers didn't make any sense. Why would you practically shut down our country without that many deaths? It didn't make sense. Our last president, a Democrat, did absolutely nothing when the swine flu ran rampant and tons of people died. I just knew that something big loomed, but I didn't know what. I speculated that China started the virus on purpose to either control their overpopulation, or hurt our economy so you'd lose the election to handsy Beaux Jaden. The Democrats whined like sore losers for the past four years," Leila explained.

"You're one smart lady. David, Zach, you should be proud of your brilliant mother," President Ace said.

"Yes, Mr. President," the boys said in unison.

"Thank you, Mr. President," Leila gushed at his lavish praise.

"Luke, did you really do all of that preparation for the end of days that Leila wrote about?" President Ace asked.

"Yes, Mr. President. I just had a bad feeling about this virus," Luke said.

"And you really foresaw the toilet paper shortage?" President Ace asked.

Luke shrugged. "I don't know how, but I did. I've slowly stockpiled supplies and guns for years. But back in September, I really kicked things up a notch."

"It's too bad you wasted all of your efforts," President Ace said.

"Wait, what? Will the world end or not?" Luke asked.

"I'll get to that." Ace turned to Leila, "I cracked up laughing over your alien invasion theory. You speculated that aliens started the virus to eliminate humans who didn't have the antibodies to the virus prior to invading us. You possess quite the overactive imagination," Ace said.

"Uh, thank you," Leila said, tentatively.

"Would you like to take a guess what the pandemic really distracted everyone from?" Mr. President asked.

"Will the world really end?" Leila asked.

"No, but a lot of people will die. I'm saving every American who voted for me. That's why I started the contest. Everyone who entered won the contest, and all the winners get to save themselves and their loved ones," Ace said.

"Our family and friends will be saved?" Relief washed through her. "But how did you know who?"

"That's why we took your phones. Pretty much everyone you keep in contact with will survive," Ace said.

"Even my girlfriend, Jane?" Zach asked.

"Yes." President Ace nodded.

"Oh, thank, God." Zach breathed an enormous sigh of relief.

"I assume Kathy Kunt won't make the cut," Leila said.

Ace held his hands together in prayer. "No, thank, God. I'll never ever have to see that treasonous, skanky bitch again." He turned to Leila. "Care to guess?"

"It's something that you've known about for a while or you wouldn't have had time to release a virus.

If the virus is even real. I'm convinced that the cruise ships have something to do with it. How else could you vacate hundreds of cruise ships unless a virus threatened the world. I predict another Great Flood," Leila speculated.

"But what causes the flood?" Ace asked.

"Holy shit! Another Great Flood is coming! But we'll survive?" Shock ran through her for accurately predicting another Great Flood.

"Mom, language," Zach chided.

Her conspiracy theories within the Great Flood scenario swam through her mind—global warming, massive hurricanes and tsunamis, solar flares, or a giant asteroid striking the planet. "Can I give you my answer once we arrive at Ace Cay?"

Ace said, "First of all, there is not an Ace Cay trip. But I'll give you a hint. It's definitely, not *Aliens* coming to our planet."

Chapter Twenty

114 days after first human dies of 61-DIVOC

Leila woke up the next morning and, for an instant, forgot her location. As she studied her surroundings and her bearings adjusted, the memory came flooding to the forefront of her mind. *I'm flying on Air Force One.*

She watched her sons sleep peacefully in their seats, which leaned all the way back to make a comfortable bed. Luke sat up and stared out of the window.

"Why didn't you wake me up?" Leila asked.

"Are you crazy? I learned a long time ago to never awaken the Kraken. You get cranky if you don't get enough sleep or fed in a timely manner." He shook his head in frustration.

"Oh, yeah." She stared at the ocean below. Dozens of tankers and cargo ships floated. "Any idea where we are at?"

Luke shrugged. "Somewhere over the ocean."

"Thanks, Einstein." Leila stared at the horizon while the sun rose behind them. "We're heading west. Are we over the Pacific Ocean?"

Shrugging, he said, "Boys, wake up! Look at this gorgeous view."

They opened their eyes and moaned with a perturbed tone. "Dad. Why did you wake us up?"

"They get their crankiness from you," Luke said.

Leila playfully smacked his chest, then stared down at the massive ocean below. As the sun rose, the early morning dawn slowly illuminated the sky, and visibility increased exponentially. Something in the distance caught her attention. "What the hell is that?" She pointed.

"What's what? I don't see anything?" Luke stared out the window.

"Oh, I forgot I'm very far sighted. It's a giant floating dock with cargo ships docked to it," Leila said. As the sun rose and lit up the sky, they grew closer to this round monstrosity floating in the middle of the ocean.

"Oh, now I see it. Cool." Luke smiled.

"How big is that thing?" Leila asked. "Those cargo ships look like toy boats compared to the big round thing."

"At least a mile in diameter," Luke said.

"Holy shit, Batman. It's a giant floating dock," Leila said.

"Oh, my, God, you're right. They engineered a way for all of the ships to survive the flood. They're expecting a giant tidal wave. That's why they made it so wide," Luke said.

They flew over the giant floating dock with several ships moored to it.

Dozens of cruise ships floated near the coast. "Look, land. Why does this look familiar? What happened to the West Coast."

David finally took an interest and stared out of the window, too. "Oh, Mom, cool. It's the VAB—Vehicle Assembly Building."

"I know what the VAB stands for, I grew up near Cape Canaveral. I'm glad you learned something from Space Camp," Leila said with a perturbed tone.

Air Force One descended. "Ladies and Gentlemen, please return to your seats and buckle your seatbelts. We land in five minutes," the pilot said over the intercom.

"What? Are we in Vandenburg, California? I didn't know California had a VAB, too."

"Yes, but the one in California looks different than the one at Cape Canaveral," Luke said.

"Dad, isn't that Launch Complex 41?" David pointed. Last summer he'd interned for Luke's company refitting the Atlas Launch Complex to also launch the new manned Vulcan rocket.

As the plane turned, a port appeared which berthed dozens of cruise ships. She recognized Jetty Park where her family camped during her childhood. "What the hell are we doing in Cape Canaveral?"

Chapter Twenty-One

114 days after first human dies of 61-DIVOC

Air Force One landed near the VAB in Cape Canaveral. Secret Service Agent Two approached them, gestured towards the port and said, "There are dozens of cruise ships in or near the port. They're all stockpiled and ready to go. Since you're a contest winner, you get to pick which cruise line you wish to board. Then your family and friends will board the same ship."

Without hesitation, Leila said, "Disney Cruise."

"Oh, Mom, no. That's so stupid." Both boys whined in unison, followed with eye rolls, sulkings and sighs of ire.

"Wow. I finally get to sail on a Disney Cruise and annoy my sons at the same time. How can this day get any better?" She grinned excitedly.

President Ace and the First Lady exited Air Force One. After a few Secret Service Agents and several more important people disembarked, the Logan Family took their turn.

Leila exited the plane and gingerly stepped onto the movable staircase. Cameras flashed, and hundreds of military personnel, NASA employees and the Press showed up to watch the mighty Air Force One deliver their beloved President Ace.

The president shook hands with a few generals before stepping behind a podium bearing the seal of the President of the United States.

With pursed lips, President Ace spoke, "Greetings, My Fellow Americans. I'm at the Kennedy Space Center in Cape Canaveral, Florida. I've just met with the top minds at NASA. Great things are happening with our new military branch—Space Force. Soon, the

United Launch Alliance, ULA, will launch their new manned rocket, the Vulcan, into space. Space X is launching all of their rockets. Blue Origins is launching, too. The International Space Station grows exponentially. Our Space Program is the best in the world. It's fantastic. Ask anyone. We'll launch all of our rockets to expand the ISS. We created lots of jobs at the Space Center. Fantastic new job numbers this month. Our Hubble Telescope sees further and further into space. It's fantastic."

Leila whispered to Luke. "They're saving all of their rockets by launching them into space and docking them at the International Space Station. Brilliant."

President Ace continued. "Once the threat of this virus is over, America will thrive once again. The Economy will bounce back quickly, and the Stock Market will grow stronger than ever. Next year will be the best year this country has ever seen. We've brought millions of gallons of dirt-cheap oil. Our reserves are overflowing, and we'll never rely on foreign countries for our oil supply ever again. Stay home, stay safe and this will all be over soon. God Bless America." With a final wave, he left the podium and shook a few more hands.

Leila stared in disbelief as she listened to their beloved President lie to the American People. Leila's mind swam with possibilities that could cause a Great Flood. Space had something to do with it. Ace confirmed that no alien invasion loomed. Since the government knew about this imminent catastrophe for nearly eight months, they had time to prepare for the second Great Flood. Leila ruled out super hurricanes or tsunamis because they'd have very little notice for those. Something President Ace said about the Hubble Telescope seeing further and further into space bridged the gap in her mind, and she realized the omniscient truth.

"Mr. President." Leila hollered and ran after President Ace. She'd probably just broken several protocols, but President Ace often ignored normal protocols.

President Ace turned and waved Leila over. He guided her a few feet away from the crowd to speak privately. "Did you figure it out?"

Nodding, she whispered, "A giant asteroid will strike the Earth, melt the glaciers and cause another Great Flood."

Ace gave her a thumbs up and said, "Bingo."

Chapter Twenty-Two

114 days after first human dies of 61-DIVOC

Leila walked the gangplank and boarded the Disney Wonder cruise ship. A Cast Member wearing vintage bellhop attire pulled two rolling luggage carts with all of their crap. Their kitties rested safely in pet carriers on top of the luggage. Sabbath murmured occasional protests.

"It's okay, kitties, you'll be out soon," Leila gushed.

"Meow." Mittens acknowledged her owner's reassurance. As if a person could truly own a cat.

The Cast Member stopped in front of a high-gloss wooden door. "Welcome to the Concierge Royal Suite."

"Sweet, a suite," Luke laughed at his own joke.

Leila shot him a disdaining scowl.

"Oh, come on, now that's funny." He tilted his head for approval.

"If you say so," she quipped.

The Cast Member opened the door to reveal an enormous suite decorated in an Art Deco decor. High-gloss wood lined the walls. A unique color scheme with grey and two shades of purple brightened the room. The design on the carpet resembled peacock feathers bursting from the grey and purple sofa. Two purple side chairs completed the living room. A flat screen television resided in high-gloss, wooden built-in cabinets.

"Wow, it's bigger than my apartment at UCF," David said.

The dining area offered an enormous bar/kitchenette area. An enormous verandah, especially by cruising standards, welcomed them. A bedroom with a king-sized bed, purple headboard and purple duvet invited her to take a nap.

"Uh, Mom, where will we sleep? I'm not sleeping on a pullout sofa with David. I don't want his 'gender fluid' on me," Zach quoted a line from the new *Vacation* movie.

The Cast Member nodded to a door off of the living room area. "It's a two-bedroom suite. The other bedroom has two oversized twin beds." The Cast Member unloaded their luggage.

"Sweet! I call the bed closest to the window," Zach hollered.

"You can't do that! Standard shotgun rules state the object must be in clear sight before calling dibs," David argued, always a stickler for the rules, but only *if* it suited him.

Zach ran to their room, stuck his head in and said, "I call it."

"Crap." David slumped in defeat.

Leila walked out onto the verandah and admired the view of Port Canaveral. Several other cruise ships berthed nearby, and hundreds of passengers boarded their way to safety.

"Hopefully the cats won't jump into the ocean, especially Little Dude." Luke referred to Sabbath who recently fell off of their dock and into the Saint John's River. Luckily, cats can swim, and he swam to the marsh and sought safety on top of a pile of reeds. Luke waded through the marsh to rescue the terrified feline.

"Speaking of kitties, let's free them from their cages." Leila opened the pet carriers and watched all three kitties reluctantly emerge and examine their new surroundings.

The Cast Member finished unloading Leila's and Luke's luggage and said, "Here's a schedule of the events and activities for the next several weeks." Then the Cast Member wheeled the second luggage cart into the boys' room.

David and Zach followed and said, "Later, gators."

"Bye, guys," Leila said without taking her eyes off of the schedule. "Disney shows, Disney movies, Character Dining and pool-side Disney trivia. There's so much to do. What should we do first?" she asked Luke.

"I'm taking a shower." Luke referred to not having showered yet after their overnight flight on Air Force One.

"Oh yeah, good idea. Then let's eat, I'm starved." Leila rubbed her belly to ward off her hunger pains.

Chapter Twenty-Three

114 days after first human dies of 61-DIVOC

The Logan Family walked into the packed main dining hall called Animator's Gallery. Giant purple mushrooms as tall as the ceiling scattered throughout the dining room. Blue and purple stained glass topped the giant mushrooms. She literally felt inside the animated film *Alice In Wonderland*. A giant Disney mural filled the large wall. Hundreds of beautifully set tables with Disney china and plush blue cushioned chairs invited them. Mexican themed decorations filled the room with festive spirit.

"Oh, yeah. I forgot that today is Cinco De Mayo." Leila vehemently needed to celebrate. She grabbed two margaritas offered by a nearby Cast Member and handed one to Luke.

They arrived at their assigned table and greeted their parents, brothers, sister-in-law and nieces. "Oh, my, God! You made it." Leila hugged her family in a joyous reunion. Everyone cried tears of happiness about reuniting after two months in quarantine.

They sat down at their large table. Leila studied the wine menu and quickly selected a bottle of Chianti. She sipped her margarita and then said, "I don't see a food menu. Do we just help ourselves to the buffet? Smells like Mexican food."

Leila sat next to her mother who also sipped a margarita. "Well, you finally get to sail on a Disney Cruise."

"I know. It's awesome. And it's free, too, because we won President Ace's contest," Leila beamed excitedly.

"Where did I go wrong?" Her mother rolled her eyes disapprovingly. Her parents *despised* Ace. But literally proved that two wrongs can make a right.

"How did you hear about the cruise ship?" Leila asked.

"Two Troops knocked on our door and told us to evacuate. They gave us one hour to pack our things. They acted like the end of the world loomed ahead," she said with an overdramatic tone.

Does her mother know the truth?

"We got a three-hour notice because we won the contest. Two Secret Service Agents picked us up, then we flew on Air Force One and met President Ace!" Leila said excitedly.

A Cast Member brought the drinks for the table and opened their bottle of wine. Leila polished off her margherita just as the Cast Member poured her a glass of Chianti.

"Well, I'm not waiting for an invitation to the buffet." Leila's father stood, grabbed his plate and walked to the buffet. If he didn't get fed dinner by six, he grew cranky. Her starving teenage sons followed their grandpa to the buffet.

Leila's mom studied the room with a worried expression. "I can't believe that we're all on a cruise ship in the middle of a pandemic."

"Mom, you do know that they created the virus to distract us, right?" Leila asked.

Leila's mother studied her with a bewildered expression. "What are you talking about? Is this another one of your crazy conspiracy theories that you're always conjuring?"

"You really don't know, do you?" Leila asked.

"Well, I read the first several chapters of your book with a pandemic, conspiracy theories and the end of the world. You and Luke have prepared for Armageddon for years," she said.

"Well, one of my crazy conspiracy theories came true! The world as we know it will end. But everyone on the cruise ships will survive," Leila said.

The shock on her mother's face unnerved her.

"Which one of your theories will actually happen?" Leila's mom asked.

Leila blurted, "A giant asteroid will strike Antarctica, melt the glaciers and cause another Great Flood!"

Chapter Twenty-Four

115 days after first human dies of 61-DIVOC

After the best night's sleep since this pandemic began, Leila awoke to the sound of the ship's fog horn. Living on the water, she quickly recognized the sound which signaled that the cruise ship would soon depart on their life saving voyage.

Already awake, Luke fiddled with his iPad. He turned to her and asked, "Room Service?"

"No way. We've been cooped up for two months! I want to socialize and see my family and friends." Leila hopped out of bed.

Leila's phone chimed. Grabbing it, she read the text from her brother—*breakfast drinks by the pool?* The Secret Service had returned their phones and electronics the night before. But the signal only reached other passengers on this ship. They'd blocked them from the outside world.

Leila showed the text to Luke who shrugged nonchalantly. "I figured you'd want to stand on the balcony while the cruise ship sails out to sea."

Leila recalled how they waved from the balcony on her one and only cruise before this during her fortieth birthday bash. "We can't. Americans would panic if they saw healthy people waving from the balconies. Remember that the rest of the world thinks the cruise ships are floating hospitals for Zinc Stink patients."

"Oh, yeah, good point," Luke said.

She donned her gator-blue bikini and teal, paisley sundress. She knocked on the boys' door before opening it. "Boys, we're headed to the pool. Wanna come?"

David and Zach slept soundly. Shrugging, she scribed a quick note and placed it on their nightstand.

Leila and Luke fed their kitties before venturing out of their enormous suite. They meandered down the hallway and found their way to the pool. She quickly spotted her brother, Damon, lounged on a chair holding a can of Bud Light. His wife, Sasha, lounged next to him wearing a cute sundress, stylish beach hat and large sunglasses.

Leila's three adorable nieces hugged her and begged her to get into the hot tub with them. Thrilled with the attention, Leila quickly placed her beach bag on a lounge chair, removed her sundress and donned her Coach sunglasses.

Luke held up the drink menu and asked, "What can I get for ya?"

While Leila's nieces dragged her to the hot tub, she turned to Luke and said, "I'll have what you're having."

While walking to the hot tub, the sight of all her friends and family flabbergasted her—aunts, uncles, first and second cousins, friends from high school and college. It felt like a wonderful combination of a family reunion, college reunion and high school reunion. She silently vowed to catch up with everyone soon.

Leila climbed into the large hot tub and relaxed in the hot water and jets. A Cast Member carrying a tray of drinks stopped by and asked, "Are you with that man over there?" He nodded towards Luke.

"Yes, I am." Leila smiled at her handsome husband.

The Cast Member handed her a Bloody Mary and said, "Let me know if I can bring you anything else."

"Thank you." Leila sipped her drink and relished in the alcohol infusion. "Ahh."

The fog horn sounded again, and the cruise ship moved.

"What's that noise?" one of her nieces asked.

"That's the fog horn to alert everyone that the cruise ship is about to sail out to sea."

From Leila's vantage point in the hot tub, she enjoyed a great view of Jetty Park and the beach, but no one on shore could see her on the top deck. As the cruise ship slowly sailed out to sea, the beach grew further and further away. A sense of foreboding filled her, and she wondered if they would ever see land again.

Chapter Twenty-Five

115 days after first human dies of 61-DIVOC

After a lazy day by the pool eating, drinking and reuniting with friends and family, Luke and Leila returned to their room. Leila said, "All of that relaxing exhausted me. I need a nap."

Luke groped her butt, his nonverbal signal that he wanted to do other things in bed besides sleep.

After entering their suite, the view from the balcony drew her like a moth to a flame. She'd expected open ocean, but not this monstrosity.

"Wow!" Leila and Luke stood awestruck on the balcony. The cruise ship slowed as it approached the giant floating dock system in the Atlantic Ocean. Several other cruise ships, cargo ships and naval ships moored to this monstrosity.

"I hope this thing works." Leila prayed.

Luke's pensive expression probably meant his brain did the math. "Yeah, the displacement is so massive that it could handle a huge wave. But I don't think the waves will get too big this far north."

"Oh, I see. Because the asteroid will supposedly strike Antarctica and melt the glaciers," Leila said while staring at the surreal sight before them.

"We may not even get waves at all, just massive rising water," he said.

"Like Hurricane Irma," Leila referred to the massive hurricane in 2017 that covered the entire state of Florida. That particular flooding in Jacksonville represented a 154-year high. They'd marked themselves safe after the storm passed through, but then the high tide rolled in, and water got within two feet of coming into their house!

"But the water will rise a gazillion times higher," Luke said with an ominous tone.

Their television automatically turned on, and the familiar, yet still annoying buzzing sound of the Emergency Broadcast System resonated throughout the cabin.

"What the hell?" Leila left the balcony and turned her full attention to the giant flat-screen television in their suite.

The Vulcan rocket launch pad appeared on the screen. It counted down, "Three, two, one. We have lift off."

"Holy Shit! That's the maiden voyage of the Vulcan rocket from Launch Complex 41! That's my baby!" Luke hollered excitedly. "Watching one of my rockets successfully launch for the first time is tantamount to watching my sons take their first steps."

"I didn't think the Vulcan was ready," Leila said with a questioning tone.

"Neither did I, but I wouldn't put it past NASA to test it with top secret launches. Especially since they're saving as many rockets as possible." Luke stared at the television screen in awe. The rocket ascended into space and got smaller and smaller as it journeyed over the Atlantic Ocean.

"I wonder if...?" Leila ran out onto the balcony.

"I just thought the same thing." Luke joined her and fiddled with his phone.

"Now you play on your phone," Leila chided.

"Chill, woman! I'm opening that launch app to track the Vulcan," he said in an annoyed tone.

"I doubt NASA would live stream it. Especially if President Ace keeps everything top secret from the rest of the world," Leila predicted.

"Oh, yeah, I didn't think about that. They locked down the app due to national security." Luke pocketed his iPhone.

Leila grinned like a kid at....

"You're going to say it, aren't you?" Luke sighed.

"'There's nothing like a good, 'I told you so.'" Leila relished the moment.

The couple stood on their balcony and studied the sky again. Passengers stood on their balconies of the other nearby cruise ships and waited for the Vulcan rocket to pass overhead.

Leila heard it before she saw it. The rocket flew overhead followed by a long trail of smoke. But instead of the normal white smoke tail, red, white and blue smoke trailed from the rocket.

With an enormous sense of pride for her country, she chanted. "USA! USA! USA!"

The other passengers quickly joined the chant. Even the cruise ships sounded their fog horns. Pretty soon, the chant caught on to the other ships. As the Vulcan rocket flew into space followed by red, white and blue smoke, millions of Americans chanted, "USA! USA! USA!"

Chapter Twenty-Six

116 days after first human dies of 61-DIVOC

Leila, Luke and the boys meandered into the Animator's Gallery for their six o'clock seating.

"Mom, can I please sit with Jane?" Zach asked, referring to his girlfriend who'd made it safely on board along with her family.

"Yes, of course. You're a grown ass man. But thanks for asking." Leila smiled at her son proudly.

They quickly found their usual table. Friends and family occupied nearly half of this side of the dining hall. A Cast Member brought everyone their pre-selected drinks. He served everyone, then proceeded to open Leila's and Luke's bottle of Chianti. He poured them each a glass before scurrying off to serve the other passengers.

"I hope they brought enough alcohol," Leila said and then took a sip of wine. She thought about the drastic change the entire world faced. She wondered how many passengers knew about the imminent asteroid strike and Great Flood. She wondered if President Ace would tell everyone onboard, or just let the passengers remain blissfully ignorant.

Several large flat screens throughout the dining hall suddenly turned on. President Ace appeared on every screen. He wore an orange NASA spacesuit and sat in some sort of space capsule.

"My Fellow Americans. Yesterday, NASA launched the maiden voyage of the Vulcan, and I flew on that rocket to the International Space Station. I will broadcast live from the ISS every day to reassure the American people that we will survive this crisis together. The Vice President is on one of the cruise ships. Most of my cabinet members are on cruise ships, but a few are here with me at the ISS," President Ace said.

Leila whispered to Luke, "Notice he didn't mention the Congresswoman, Kathy Kunt."

Ace continued, "This space station is absolutely incredible. NASA did a fantastic job to nearly double its size in the last year. American technology proves far superior than the rest of the world. Our scientists are fantastic. Our military is fantastic. Americans are fantastic.

"As most of you have probably realized by now, something much bigger is really happening. In less than eight months, the United States Navy built two enormous floating docks. One is off of the coast of Cape Canaveral, Florida. And the other is off the coast of Vandenburg Air Force base in California. These floating dock systems accommodate nearly every large ship in the world. We even purchased all of the ships around the world. Battle ships, air craft carriers, naval destroyers, cruise ships and cargo ships are securely tethered to the floating dock systems. We're saving all of our jets and rockets, too. We've managed to save as many Americans as possible. Millions of Americans will survive."

"Just the ones who voted for him," Leila snickered.

"Our nuclear submarines protect the waters around us. Our cargo ships have enough food and supplies to last us for years. We're catching fish in the ocean and growing fruits and vegetables on these tanker ships. We've stocked thousands and thousands of livestock which we can breed and eat. We'll never go hungry.

"In a few days, an asteroid will strike Antarctica. We are far enough away to survive the tidal waves and tsunamis. However, once the asteroid strikes our planet, it will melt the glaciers and raise the water levels over two thousand feet. Like the biblical Great Flood, these ships will survive like Noah's Ark. The American people will live on. Thank you and God Bless America," President Ace said.

Chapter Twenty-Seven

117 days after first human dies of 61-DIVOC

Leila shot up in bed the next morning to loud rumbles and a shaking cruise ship. It reminded her of her childhood home in Titusville, Florida. With its close proximity to Cape Canaveral, all of the windows shook for several minutes every time the Space Shuttle launched.

Luke got out of bed and ran to the balcony, but he didn't open the sliding glass door. Leila joined him and asked, "What the hell is that?"

Zach and David opened the door to their room and ran to join them at the sliding glass door. "What the fuck is that?" Zach asked.

"Language," Leila scolded her son.

"Oops, sorry, Mom," he said with a remorseful tone.

The monstrous floating dock structure shook and wobbled. Large waves rose from the south. Not the crashing kind, but the kind you float over.

"The asteroid struck the Earth," Leila said with a calming tone. She didn't want her sons to know that anxiety raced through her veins because she didn't know if they'd survive this cataclysmic moment in history.

"I thought we had a few more days before the asteroid struck," David said.

"He probably told us that so we wouldn't freak out like Mom is now." Zach pointed to her hands which shook like a Parkinson's patient.

"Well, you know me. I freak out about everything, especially teaching ya'll how to drive." Leila tried to downplay her fear.

From the southern horizon, dozens of large waves floated towards them and grew bigger and bigger.

Fearful, Leila turned to Luke and said, "You said we'd only experience small waves because of our distance from Antarctica."

"That doesn't make any sense," David, the future Aerospace Engineer said. "Think of throwing a pebble into a pond. The ripples get bigger the further out they go."

Oh shit! Leila didn't want to say it out loud because the big waves terrified her.

A calm voice resonated throughout the sound system. "For your safety, please put on a life jacket and buckle yourselves onto the sofas and chairs."

"What the hell?" Leila asked.

Luke walked over to the sofa. He tried to move it, but it wouldn't budge. Being a typical engineer, he knelt on the floor and examined underneath the sofa. "It's bolted down. This sucker won't budge." He reached underneath the cushions. "Aha. There are actually seatbelts here. Come on, take a seat."

Leila sat on the sofa and buckled up. "Huh, at least we have a view of the balcony so we can see what's coming."

"Not sure if that's a good thing or not. Sometimes ignorance is bliss." Luke sat down next to her and buckled his seatbelt.

"Come on boys." Leila patted the empty cushion next to her.

"I'm hungry." Zach rubbed his tummy.

"Go nuke some popcorn. We can pretend that we're watching a horror film." Leila chuckled as she downplayed their precarious situation.

The microwave dinged, and Zach pulled out the bag of popcorn and opened it. The buttery aroma permeated the room.

"Ahh, that smells wonderful. Go ahead and nuke another bag. We don't know how long this will last," Leila ordered.

"And get four beers out of the fridge while you're up," Luke ordered.

Leila shot him a dirty look, but then nonverbally applauded his brilliance.

"Cool." David grabbed a four pack of Guinness and carried it to the sofa.

Zach brought both bags of popcorn and handed one to his parents before buckling up.

The first wave approached, maybe twenty feet high. The far end of the floating dock and its corresponding ships rose up over the wave. As it got closer to the crest of the wave, the next section of the floating dock rose up and over the wave. The first set of ships floated successfully to the other side to await the next wave.

They braced themselves for their imminent rise up the wave. Twenty feet paled in comparison to a ship nearly one-thousand-feet long. As they rose up with the ship, the incline in their room caused a noticeable imbalance.

"This isn't so bad. It's kind of cool actually," Zach said.

Don't speak too soon. Leila silently scolded her youngest son. "I hope these waves slowly move us north and further away from the epicenter."

As they reached the top of the wave, the first set of ships already rose on the next and even larger wave. Mentally calculating the distance, she figured that this monstrous floating dock contraption would float over several waves at once. They floated down their first wave with the same incline of the initial rise, just in the opposite direction. The brilliantly engineered floating dock provided enough displacement to keep everyone afloat.

Dozens of jets flew above, heading south to presumably assess the severity of the incoming waves.

"I guess the planes are safer in the sky than on an aircraft carrier," Leila said. *What the hell do they know that we don't!*

The next wave rose them up to the crest and revealed bigger waves headed towards them. *Holy Shit!*

Leila futilely attempted to hide her fear. Panic rose in her chest, and she felt like she couldn't breathe. Her hands shook uncontrollably, and she prayed for their lives. Luke squeezed her hand reassuringly; but her heart raced, and blood boiled in her veins.

"Mom, chill, stop freaking out," Zach ordered.

Leila nodded, wrapped her arms around herself and took slow, deep breaths. Without looking, she felt the next wave raise them up, lift them over the crest and then float back down again. "I wish I had Dramamine."

"They gave you that patch for sea sickness," Luke said.

"But that's nowhere near enough. I feel like I've ridden Space Mountain ten times in a row." Leila felt her stomach's imminent rejection of the popcorn. She knelt over her knees and heaved her guts out all over the gray and purple carpet. Luckily, she didn't puke all over herself because they floated down the wave.

"Ewe, Mom! That's so gross!" The boys both hollered.

"You gonna live?" Luke asked with a sarcastic tone.

Nodding, Leila said, "Actually, I feel better. I usually do after I puke."

"Tossing cookies," Zach said and gestured as if he literally threw cookies into the air.

The gesture reminded her of their trip to the Blue Ridge Mountains in North Carolina. The winding mountain roads made her car sick, and Luke barely pulled over in time to let her vomit on the side of the road. Little boys watching their mother throw up fascinated them. They named every imaginable metaphor for throwing up—puking, vomiting, blowing chunks, ralphing and hurling. But Zach thought tossing cookies the funniest of them all.

"I'm okay, but I can't drink this beer." Leila handed it over to Luke who gladly took it off of her hands. "Boys, when we reach the calm bottom, please get me a Ginger Ale out of the refrigerator."

"Sure." David studied the wave pattern, waited until they floated back down, then he got up and retrieved a Ginger Ale for his ill mother.

"Thanks, David." Leila opened the can, took a small sip and instantly felt better as the cool bubbles and ginger settled her stomach. As the bigger waves approached, she liked watching the ships on the southern end of the floating dock float safely over first.

"I feel like I'm on a ride at Disney." Luke held his hands up over his head like rollercoaster riders do.

Leila appreciated his levity while they got through this. But huge waves loomed omnisciently.

The biggest wave yet lifted the first ship up parallel to the enormous swell. As it neared the top, the ship capsized.

Chapter Twenty-Eight

117 days after first human dies of 61-DIVOC

"Holy Shit! Did you see that?" Zach pointed to the enormous ship which capsized before it floated over the top of a hundred-foot-tall wave.

Leila closed her eyes, performed the sign of the cross and silently repeated the Hail Mary prayer. The next wave lifted them up while she kept her eyes closed. She never stopped praying. Relief washed through her with that now familiar feeling of floating over the precipice of the wave.

"Mom, look!" Zach hollered.

Leila shook her head and kept her eyes closed. "I don't want to see anything else bad."

"Mom, it's good," David said.

Leila tentatively opened one eye, then the other. The once capsized ship now floated in its original, upright position. "Huh?"

"It must've flipped back over when it went down the wave," Zach said.

"That's a good sign. But those poor people who went underwater. I hope everyone is okay." Leila worried.

"You'd be surprise how thick this glass is." Luke pointed to the thick sliding glass door leading to their balcony.

"Hopefully they kept the glass door closed." Leila shuddered at the horrific notion of being capsized, even temporarily.

"Even if a little water got in, it only capsized for a minute," Luke said reassuringly.

"I hope they wore their seat belts." Leila double checked her tightly secured seatbelt. "You'd be surprised how many idiots don't wear a seatbelt."

"Or use a turn signal or stop at stop signs," Zach referred to all the terrible drivers he discovered since he learned how to drive.

The next and even bigger wave picked up the first ship. As it rose up towards the top, it capsized again.

"Is that the only ship that keeps capsizing?" Leila asked.

Luke and the boys studied the countless other ships moored to the monstrous floating dock. "It's too far to see all of the ships, but that's the only one I've seen capsized."

"Maybe they didn't secure that particular ship properly to the floating dock," she speculated.

"Or a security tether broke. Quality control. That's why I'll always have a job. People make mistakes." Luke shook his head incredulously.

As they floated up and down the next wave, Leila's anxiety subsided. Focusing on the positive, she said, "At least it's not hurricane season. Can you imagine being out here in a category five storm?" She referred to the highest-level hurricane with winds over 156 miles per hour.

"Oh, my, God! We'd all be dead." Zach rolled his eyes.

"Except for President Ace in space," Leila corrected.

"Can you imagine if Ace lost the 2016 Election to that treasonous, communist dick?" Luke shook his head, obviously grateful for the favorable election results.

"We'd definitely die." Leila shuddered at the nightmarish notion. Thinking of how much worse things could've been eased her anxiety.

"Hey, look. That ship turned right side up again." David pointed.

Leila studied the corrected ship. As they rode the next wave over the top, she counted only three more big waves headed towards them. "Guys look. Only three waves left!" Leila said, excitedly. *Holy shit! We just might survive this thing after all!*

Chapter Twenty-Nine

117 days after first human dies of 61-DIVOC

They floated over the last three waves without problems. In the distance, several jets flew towards the nearby aircraft carrier.

"I guess it's safe for the jets to land," Leila said.

"Uh, but they're not landing." Zach pointed as the jets flew over the aircraft carrier without slowing down.

A loud rumbling sound resonated from the horizon.

"What the hell?" David asked.

The windows on the ship rattled like her parents' house whenever a rocket launched from nearby Cape Canaveral.

"Dad, it sounds like the river rapids when we went white-water rafting at Camp Summit." Zach referred to the summer when Luke accompanied both of their sons on a high-adventure Boy Scout camp. They shot guns, threw axes, ziplined, biked, skateboarded and white-water rafted.

A shiver shot through Leila's spine, and her skin prickled with goose bumps.

The television turned on, and an announcement resonated. "Attention all passengers. Please remain in your seats and keep your seatbelts and floatation devices secure."

The sound of a waterfall grew louder and louder. Luke grabbed his binoculars and squinted as he peered through the small oculi.

"How bad is it?" Leila asked, fearing the answer.

Luke handed her the binoculars. "See for yourself."

Leila grabbed the binoculars. Taking a deep breath, she slowly exhaled and braved a peek at whatever the hell loomed. Incredulity filled her as panic rose in her chest again. A massive amount of water rushed towards them. It resembled water rushing out of a broken damn and flooding the valley below. *Holy Shit!*

"Mom, let us see." David rudely yanked the binoculars away from her and peered through. His expression turned stunned. The color quickly drained from his face as he handed the binoculars to Zach.

Zach peered through and repeated his brother's stunned expression and loss of color. "Holy shit!"

"Ya'll are the physics experts, but I'm guessing the first rippling waves originated from the asteroid striking the Earth. But this monstrosity generated from melting glaciers. It's like a tsunami, except the water didn't recede beforehand," Leila said.

"Yep," Luke said.

They all held hands.

"Mom, what should we do?" Zach asked.

"We pray. *Hail Mary, full of Grace, The Lord is with thee. Blessed art thou among women, and blessed is the fruit of thy womb, Jesus. Holy Mary, Mother of God, pray for us sinners now, and at the hour of death. Amen.*"

The family of four recited the prayer over and over again. Presumably, every human on this and the other ships prayed for dear life, too.

Leila daringly opened her eyes and assessed the proximity of the giant, pummeling wave. It approached the first set of ships at the southern edge of the giant floating dock. Now that she'd seen the imminent danger, her morbid curiosity sank in, and she couldn't keep her eyes off of the impending macabre.

The tidal wave struck the first ship and knocked it on its side. The wave covered the ship and moved on to its next victim. The wave stuck again, and the second ship turned on its side before the tidal wave completely covered it. Terrifying screams echoed from the submerged ships.

"How long is that wave?" Leila asked.

Luke shrugged. "I can't tell. It's too tall to see the end."

Leila braced herself for the imminent thrashing they'd endure. At least they'd be on the top side when their ship capsized.

White rapids neared their ship. Water struck the entire broad side and knocked it to a ninety-degree angle and covered the ship. Now they laid on the sofa instead of sitting on it. Swirling water rushed above them. At least the windows and sliding glass door held, and no water entered their cabin. The ship moved with the wave as its force pushed them along.

"As long as we don't die, this is actually kind of cool," Zach said.

The water continued to flow above them. She felt like a fish in an aquarium staring out of the glass to see the outside world. "I'm shocked that glass didn't break," Leila said with an incredulous tone.

"It wouldn't surprise me if they reinforced all the cruise ships with thicker glass windows and doors," Luke said.

The white-water rapids carried them northward at what felt like 60 knots, nearly 70 mph. The rapids reminded her of the Kali River Rapids ride at Animal Kingdom at Walt Disney World. Only this ride moved much faster, and water completely covered them. But they had no idea how long this water ride would last, nor their fate.

Leila studied the sliding glass door and marveled at how well they'd sealed it. Pointing, she said, "I'm surprised water isn't seeping through the sliding glass door."

"Mom, don't jinx it!" Zach hollered.

Just as he said it, water sprayed through the seams of the sliding glass door.

"Well there ya go; now this is all your fault, Mom," David shamed her.

Leila wondered, if the seal broke on their door, how many other doors suffered the same fate?

"Why didn't they make retractable steel walls like they did in the movie *2012*?" Zach asked, referring to the end of days movie where solar flares caused a Great Flood.

"Because the movie *2012* is fictional," Leila said.

"Really? This seems pretty close, only we had an asteroid instead of solar flares," Zach said.

"He's got you there, Mom," David said.

Water slowly sprayed into their cabin. Always the optimist, Leila said, "Well, look at the bright side. At least we're on top of the ship. The water won't stay in this cabin for long."

"Yeah, but if the ship takes on too much water, we'll sink," Luke warned.

"We're still moored to the floating raft. Won't that keep us afloat?' Leila asked.

"Let's hope," Luke said.

Leila held her hands together in prayer, "Let's pray."

Chapter Thirty

118 days after first human dies of 61-DIVOC

Leila startled awake. *How the hell did I sleep through that?* With no electricity, the dark cabin screamed doom and gloom. Water still flowed above them as they rode the white-water wave, luckily their pace definitely slowed.

Luke sat next to her fiddling with his iPad. The boys snored on the couch. *Dem boys can sleep through anything.*

"What time is it?" Leila asked.

"Almost dawn," Luke said.

"How did I sleep so long? And why did you let me sleep through all of that?" Leila asked.

"I've learned to never awaken the Kraken. Besides, I would've wakened you if we needed to take action." Luke fiddled with his iPad without looking up.

"Do you even have a signal?" she asked.

"Just the ship's WIFI. The bright lights keep me alert."

"Don't tell me you stayed up all night?" she asked.

Nodding, he said, "Pretty much. Protecting my family."

"Awe, how valiant. My knight in shining armor," Leila gushed. "Did we slow down."

"Yep." Pointing towards the window, he added, "We're pretty close to the surface. The morning sun lit the cabin. It surprises me that we're still underwater given the buoyancy of all these ships tethered to the floating dock." Luke said with a pensive expression. As if he mentally calculated the thermodynamics.

"Hopefully, the worst is almost over." Leila studied the surface, probably only fifteen feet above them.

A thunderous noise reverberated throughout the cabin.

"Oh, shit! Boys, wake up!" Luke hollered.

"Huh? What?" The boys asked.

"Brace yourselves. The ride is not over yet," Luke said.

"You just calculated everything in your head," Leila said, not asked.

"Yep." Luke nodded, obviously proud of his genius IQ.

The thunder grew louder, and a strong whooshing force pulled them up. The ship slowly rotated two different ways simultaneously. The ninety-degree angle on its side slowly corrected itself, and the bow of the ship headed towards the surface at a forty-five-degree angle. They no longer lay on the couch, but sat on the couch leaning sideways.

It felt like riding a roller coaster, but instead of gravity pushing them, buoyancy pulled them. The surface grew closer and closer, and the morning sun's rays shone, illuminating the cabin. As the ship breached the surface, it cut through the water like a submarine surfacing abruptly from the depths of the ocean. It almost felt as if they'd caught air on part of the ship. The ship lurched forward with enough force that the ship floated upright in its proper position.

They all unbuckled their seatbelts and walked to the balcony. They opened the doors and a wonderful sight greeted them—the surface. The floating dock and all the ships returned upright. They'd survived the pandemic, the asteroid and the Great Flood. Now they must wait. Wait to live or wait to die. But at least they all survived together.

The boys asked in unison, "Mom, what's for breakfast?"

Chapter Thirty-One

118 days after first human dies of 61-DIVOC

Not knowing what to expect Luke, Leila and their sons arrived at the main dining room. Knocked over chairs and tables littered the room, but the buffet remained intact bolted to the floor.

Everyone else had the same idea. All starving, but also curious to ascertain how everyone else onboard fared the last tumultuous twenty-four hours.

"Breakfast consists of making your own sandwiches to go until we get the dining room and kitchen back in order," a Cast Member said as he picked up another overturned chair and returned it to its rightful position.

Little arms wrapped around Leila's waist in a big hug. Leila knew the identity of her tiny hugger before she even looked down to ascertain her accuracy. Her youngest niece hugged her like she'd never see her favorite aunt again. Leila knew from experience that she couldn't pry off her niece because she always clung to her like scotch tape.

Instead, Leila bent down, wrapped Leila's arms around her neck and picked her up to hug her protectively. Although eleven-years-old, she only weighed about fifty pounds. "You okay, Leila?" Leila asked.

"That scared me. I'm glad everyone is okay now," Niece Leila said.

Leila hugged her niece tightly before setting her down. "Those huge waves scared me, too. But I just thought of it as a super-fast and fun Disney rollercoaster and that made me less scared," Leila explained. Then a saddening notion struck her—Disney gone forever!

Zach quickly found his girlfriend, Jane, and hugged her like he thought he'd never see her again.

Brother Damon appeared carrying a blue aluminum bottle of Bud Light. Leave it to her bro to find a stash of beer after their ship capsized.

"Well, that didn't take you long," Leila said sarcastically before hugging her slightly younger Irish Twin. Although not actually twins, that's what the Irish called siblings born less than one year apart.

Their parents appeared, and everyone hugged. Then dad bitched about his starvation. Without waiting for an invitation to the buffet of different breads and cold cuts, he took it upon himself to make two sandwiches.

Mom rolled her eyes with an annoyed expression.

Studying the crowd in the dining hall, Leila presumed that everyone on their ship made it through the flash flood unscathed.

They quickly followed Dad's lead and made sandwiches. Since they couldn't eat in the dining hall, they meandered out to the pool area, now full of ocean water. They walked to the railing and studied the enormous floating contraption with hundreds of ships still moored in place.

"Mom, look. One of the ships is missing!" David pointed to where the troubled ship once berthed.

"Ah, that's sad. Hopefully they wore life preservers and jumped overboard," Leila said with an optimistic tone.

Luke whispered, "Even if they did jump overboard in time, the strength of that flash flood would be nearly impossible to survive." He grimaced at the horrific notion.

"Hopefully that ship held Kathy Kunt," David said.

"It's pronounced Koont, like the *coon* in rac*coon*," Luke corrected sarcastically, referring to how the presumably deceased Congresswoman changed the pronunciation of her name so people wouldn't call her Madame Kunt, pronounced like cunt.

"I highly doubt she even made it onboard any of the ships. President Ace said he'd never have to see her again. He jokingly promised to use her as chum, but we all know he meant it," Leila said.

Dozens of helicopters and jets returned to their respective air craft carriers. They'd obviously survived the Great Flood since they flew safely in the sky. Luckily, they had enough fuel to stay in the air.

Leila studied the empty berth on the floating dock where the doomed ship once floated. Something caught her attention, and she peered more inquisitively at the floating dock's perimeter.

Even with her excellent, long-distance vision, Leila squinted with the morning sun's rays reflecting off of the water. Tiny white creatures moved in the water. Then these creatures climbed up onto the floating dock, and elation filled her.

"Look! Survivors!" Leila pointed to the passengers wearing white life preservers slowing emerging from the water and climbing safely onboard the floating dock.

"Where?" Luke asked with a doubtful tone.

"Oooh, oooh, oooh! I see them, Mom." David pointed excitedly.

"'Seems highly illogical, Jim,'" Damon quoted Spock from Star Trek.

Then Luke obviously spotted dozens of survivors emerging. He turned to Leila and asked, "You're going to say it, aren't you?"

Leila beamed triumphantly and said, "I told you so!"

After a few jovial chuckles, Leila relived the floating waves and white-water rapids in her mind.

The floating waves reminded her of the giant wave pool at Disney's Blizzard Beach and the white-water rapids reminded her of the harsh rushing wave at Disney's Typhoon Lagoon. She'd spent enough time at those two water parks with her sons over the last twelve years to recognize the similarity to the waves of the last twenty-four hours. Disney's waves proved much smaller and less intense. A horrific realization filled her with terror—Disney artificially generated those waves.

Chapter Thirty-Two

119 days after first human dies of 61-DIVOC

"Great dinner." Luke finished his filet mignon with a hefty sip of chianti.

"We're getting fat on this ship." Leila sucked in her gut and ate the last bite of scrumptious steak.

They enjoyed their first dinner at Triton's restaurant. Trying something other than Tianna's Palace and Animator's Gallery felt refreshing.

Helicopters and jets returned to nearby aircraft carriers. They'd flown all day, presumably searching for land.

"I wonder if they found land." Leila swigged the rest of her wine and seriously contemplated taking a peek at the dessert buffet.

"Mom, would you like us to bring you something chocolate from the dessert buffet?" Zach asked, obviously reading her mind.

"Ah, what a thoughtful son I have," Leila gushed. "Chocolate sounds marvelous, thank you."

Zach and David left the table to forage something sweet. Luke studied the drink menu with a pensive expression.

Knowing her husband of twenty-five years all too well, she read his mind. "Can't decide on an after-dinner drink?" she asked.

"Tequila or port?" he asked.

"Get what you want, but I'm in the mood for champagne." Leila smiled.

"What are we celebrating?" Luke asked.

"Surviving the second Great Flood." Her *duh* implied in her tone.

"Sounds good to me." Luke waived the Cast Member over and asked. "Can you please bring us a bottle of Dom Perignon."

"Certainly, Sir," the Cast Member said.

David and Zach reappeared carrying two dessert plates each.

"Your favorite, Mom, chocolate mousse pie," Zach said.

"Ah, thank you." Leila studied the scrumptious chocolate mousse and silently vowed to diet once they disembarked.

"Dad, here's a slice of cheese cake," David said.

The Cast Member returned with a bottle of Dom Perignon and popped the cork. Then he poured four glasses of champagne.

Other diners followed their lead, and a dozen more champagne corks popped in the restaurant.

"Mmm. It's so good, just one more bite and I'm done." Leila took one last bite and then pushed the dessert plate away.

"Let's walk this dinner off on the deck." Luke pushed his chair out.

Leila topped off all four champagne flutes and said, "Let's finish our champagne while we stroll along the promenade."

Everyone stood, and they walked outside to stroll along the deck. Although no one said it, everyone searched for dry land and waited for the proverbial olive branch.

Something floated on the horizon. Hope filled her as she prayed to see land. "Look, it might be land!" Leila pointed excitedly.

Skeptical, Luke studied the horizon. "Something large is floating. Land doesn't move with the waves."

"Dad's right, Mom," David said.

"Ya'll and your physics and thermodynamics," Leila said, miffed that she didn't find land. *What could it be? Trash?* Most likely, she'd heard millions of empty plastic water bottles floated in the ocean.

"Mom, do you see those moving specks above whatever floats out there?" Zach asked.

"Yeah. It looks like... Oh, my, God! It must be land because birds are flying above and sitting on whatever floats in the water. If it's not land, what could it possibly be?" she asked.

"Maybe it's a big whale that didn't survive the flash flooding," Luke speculated.

"Ewe, gross. I don't want to see that." Leila grimaced.

"Yep, those birds are definitely frenzy feeding over something," Luke said.

"But surely there must be land nearby if we see birds," Leila speculated.

"Not necessarily. They could've taken to the sky when the floodwaters hit. Poor things probably flew for hours before they found somewhere to land."

A bird flew closer to the ship and definitely carried something in its mouth.

Leila lit up with excitement. "What are the odds of a bird bringing an olive branch just like one did to Noah's Ark?"

"Don't get your hopes up. Whatever is in that bird's mouth is round with something hanging off of it," Luke said.

The bird flew directly over them, then dropped the mystery object onto the deck.

Dozens of passengers, who'd also watched the bird with hopeful curiosity, flocked to the object on deck.

"What is that?" Luke asked.

"Cool," David and Zach said in unison.

Leila finally peeked at the mystery object. Definitely *not* an olive branch. A human eyeball stared at her!

Chapter Thirty-Three

120 days after first human dies of 61-DIVOC

Leila screamed in her sleep as she woke up from her nightmare—human eyeballs on the ship's deck. Night terrors occurred when she tried to scream in her nightmare so hard that she actually screamed in real life.

"Jesus, Leila! Your scream frightened poor Mittens," Luke said with a groggy tone because her scream obviously woke him up, too. He rolled over and fell back asleep.

She rolled onto her side and reflected on her dream. She'd dreamt that she floated on waves at Blizzard Beach, but the waves at the water park eventually floated her to the ocean. Then the waves grew bigger and bigger, like the ones they'd floated over in the second Great Flood. In her dream, she screamed for help before she woke up.

Thinking of the giant man-made waves floating her out to sea conjured another conspiracy theory. She'd previously speculated that terrorists artificially generated hurricanes and tsunamis. *Could giant waves and white-water rapids like they'd just experienced be man-made, too?* She tried to shake off the horrific notion, but her mind kept spinning. The implications terrified her. In addition to the government either starting or faking a pandemic, *did the United States government and military fake an asteroid? Why would they do that? Did the United States just commit mass genocide to reduce overpopulation?* Then she recalled Hitler and his genocide of millions of Jews during WWII.

Leila shrugged off the demonic notion. Her mind truly warped to even consider that her beloved president could murder billions of humans. A conspiracy within a conspiracy within another conspiracy felt bat shit crazy. She decided not to even share her newest theory because Luke would promptly commit her to a loony bin.

Sitting up in bed, she mentally tucked her crazy thoughts away and realized that they never learned what floated in the ocean because it grew dark.

Leila got out of bed and immediately walked to the balcony. Their new routine each morning—scan the horizon for dry land.

Birds flew closer to the ships, and the mystery mass floated next to the gigantic floating dock.

Leila stared in horror once the mystery revealed itself. Not dry land, not trash, not dead whales.

Luke joined her on the balcony and grimaced.

Even the boys stood on the balcony this early.

A breeze blew towards them with a putrid odor of rot and death.

Dead bodies floated in the ocean, thousands of them.

"Oh, God! That's so sad and disgusting." Leila performed the sign of the cross and said a silent prayer for the lost lives.

The boys stared with macabre interest, but respectfully remained silent.

All of the ships along the perimeter of the floating dock lowered life boats to collect human remains.

"Why collect all of the bodies? What in the hell do they plan to do with all of those dead people?" Leila asked.

"Burn them, I suppose," Luke speculated.

"Where? Oh, wait. I heard cruise ships have morgues because tons of old people cruise all of the time, even when they're 100," Leila said.

"Maybe. Or maybe they'll stack them on life boats and burn them at sea like the Vikings did," Luke said.

"That sounds more humane than letting them rot in the ocean and or eaten by birds and sharks," Leila said.

Several life boats lowered into the water. Two Cast Members occupied each life boat. Once the boats hit the water, each Cast Member used a pole with a giant hook to pull the bodies onboard. Once they got each body onboard the life boat, they respectfully laid each corpse out and placed their hands over their chests like they do at funeral homes. As they laid out each body, the Cast Members removed their jewelry.

"Ewe, yuk. They can't possibly pay those people enough." Leila grimaced.

Each boat stacked about a hundred corpses and nearly sank from the weight.

With a lost appetite, the Logan Family skipped breakfast altogether.

The television automatically turned on, and President Ace appeared on the screen.

"Greetings, My Fellow Americans. I'm thrilled that most of the Americans on the cruise ships survived this Great Flood. It's fantastic. Our great country, technology and military helped us survive this catastrophe. Our NASA guys with the Hubble Telescope discovered the asteroid eight months ago. Our great military, especially the Navy, coordinated this massive undertaking to design and build two gigantic floating docks. I viewed the asteroid striking Earth from the ISS. An absolutely horrible event. It truly is a miracle that so many Americans survived. As you may have noticed, billions of humans did not survive. To honor their memory and respect their remains, we will hold a giant funeral service for the bodies we recovered from the ocean. The funeral service commences tomorrow at dusk. But before then, I will return to Earth on the Vulcan capsule. More fantastic news, our jets scouted the planet for land and found it. The tops of the major mountain ranges are above water. It's enough land to rebuild the United States of America. But now our United States won't be just in America, it will be all over the world. God bless the United States of Earth."

A chill shivered Leila. *The United States of Earth.* As much as Leila loved her country and her president, the notion of one person commanding the entire planet terrified her.

Chapter Thirty-Four

121 days after first human dies of 61-DIVOC

"Where will the capsule land exactly?" Leila asked, then sipped a glass of Bordeaux. Since they loved Triton's so much the night before, they decided to come back and try a different entrée. Leila ordered rack of lamb, and Luke ordered roasted duck.

"I think we'll see it from here." Luke popped an escargot into his mouth. "What are the boys doing?"

"Taking a nap. In fact, Sabbath and Pumpkin slept with Zach, and Mittens slept with David. I'm sure they'll just hang with their friends." Leila ate another escargot, then dunked a crostini into the remaining garlic butter served with the escargot.

"Lazy teenage boys." Luke smirked. "I'll text them to watch the Vulcan capsule return to Earth."

"Hey, look who it is." Leila pointed to her brother, Damon. He sipped a Bud Light and sat at their table.

Leila's mini me gave her a big hug and asked. "Can I please sit next to you, Aunt Leila?"

"Of course." She relished the attention of her doting eleven-year-old niece.

"Where's your other girls?" Leila asked.

"Sasha and Rebecca went shopping, and Malia is hanging out with her boyfriend," Damon said.

"Damon, tell me all about the capsule landing," Leila said.

"Hey, what am I, chopped liver?" Luke asked. His tone rang with ire and understandably so. He worked on the Vulcan launch complex, after all.

"Oh, yeah. Sorry. It's just that Damon worked at NASA for years. He knows everything you *never* wanted to know about the Space Program," Leila quipped.

"The Vulcan is similar to the Apollo capsule. Only the Vulcan capsule is bigger. It simply parachutes into the ocean and floats until a boat retrieves the capsule and the astronauts," Damon explained.

"It amazes me that they calculate exactly where they wish the capsule to land, and then make it happen. It's miraculous that they did it over fifty years ago," Leila said with a surprised tone.

A Cast Member arrived and asked, "Can I get you anything?"

Damon said, "I'll have the Chateaubriand Filet and another Bud Light." He shook his empty bottle.

"And what would you like to eat, young lady?" the Cast Member asked.

Niece Leila said with the sweetest voice and most adorable smile, "I'll have pasta and a coke."

The television screen in the restaurant turned on. WAOK News broadcasted from one of the cruise ships. A picture of the Vulcan capsule appeared on the screen viewing the Earth from the capsule. WAOK News Commentator, Lilly Allen Garrison, said, "This breaking news just in. The Vulcan capsule successfully reentered the Earth's atmosphere and will soon land in the Atlantic Ocean."

"When do they pull the chute?" Leila asked. "That capsule is dropping pretty fast."

"They don't want to pull it too soon because the wind could blow the capsule off course. But hopefully they'll pull the chute soon," Damon said.

"Yeah, we don't want the leader of our world to die." That notion chilled Leila.

The Vulcan capsule slowed down, and Lilly Allen Garrison said, "The parachute successfully deployed, we will now go live to the USS Florida who will retrieve the capsule and President Ace."

The screen changed from the capsule to the USS Florida.

"I see it." Leila pointed.

"Where? I don't see it on the screen," Luke said.

"No, silly, I see it through the window." Leila pointed towards the window at the white parachute floating the descending capsule.

They all stared at the capsule floating towards open water. Once the capsule disappeared in the sky, they turned their attention back to the television with two camera angles on the screen—one from the Vulcan capsule cam and one from the USS Florida.

Leila quickly performed the sign of the cross as the capsule plunged safely back on Earth.

Chapter Thirty-Five

121 days after first human dies of 61-DIVOC

The Logan Family, along with three thousand passengers and crew of the Disney Wonder, stood on the decks of the ship. Everyone wore black to mourn the billions of human lives lost during the second Great Flood. Although the Navy only recovered a few thousand bodies, this massive funeral represented the unrecovered humans, too.

As the last lingering light of the recently set sun disappeared from the horizon, the jumbo television screen turned on, and President Ace appeared. "Greetings, My Fellow Americans. As many of you witnessed, I safely landed back on Earth. Now I'll turn it over to Pope Francis who will officiate the Funeral Mass."

Leila shot Luke a shocked expression. "Holy Shit! The Pope!"

"You're going to hell now," Luke chastised.

"I guess it makes sense to save the Pope or we'd all be dead from the Great Flood." Leila shrugged.

"Shhh, Mom. You're not supposed to talk in church," Zach scolded. Grinning to get back at his mother for shushing him many times in the past during Mass.

A picture of the enormous altar at St. Peter's Basilica in the Vatican appeared on the screen.

"Wait? How is the Vatican not underwater?" Luke asked.

"It's probably just an old picture they used as a backdrop. He's probably on one of these cruise ships," Leila speculated.

"Mom, I see the Pope!" David hollered excitedly.

Leila studied the screen and asked, "Where? I don't see him."

David turned her body sideways and pointed. "He's in front of the ship's chapel with the Processional.

Awestruck, she said, "Holy shit! That's definitely him. Let's quietly head to the chapel before all of the other passengers notice him, too."

Leila quickly led the way to the chapel with determination to see her third Pope in person. On their Italian honeymoon in 1994, she and Luke watched Pope John Paul II give a Sunday blessing from his window to a packed St. Peter's Square. In 1999 Luke and Leila attended Midnight Mass at Christmas in St. Peter's Square where they glimpsed Pope John Paul II with the Processional outside the basilica. And in 2008 they attended Midnight Mass on Christmas *inside* St. Peter's Basilica with their sons and saw Pope Benedict XVI. In fact, David and Zach had their literal First Communions at St. Peter's. Technically, they should've waited until their official First Communion at their Catholic Church once they completed their religious classes, but they couldn't let their sons miss the opportunity to have their very First Communion at St. Peter's Basilica in the Vatican.

They entered the chapel after the Processional, a big *no no* in Mass etiquette. "I wish I'd known that the Disney Wonder carried the Pope, then I wouldn't have worried so much after the asteroid struck," Leila said.

They quickly slid into a pew near the front of the chapel. After standing, kneeling, and sitting down several times, Mass went by quickly. They even received the Sacrament of Communion from the Pope himself. Leila felt truly blessed, even on this sad occasion. They left the chapel after the Pope and his Processional.

Luke snapped his fingers and said, "Awe, shucks."

"What is it?" she asked.

"We forgot to ask the Pope if he shits in the woods," Luke referred to the two crisscrossed idioms—"Does a bear shit in the woods?" And "Is the Pope Catholic?"

"Now you're going to hell." Leila placed her bent index fingers on top of her head like little devil horns from an episode of *Seinfeld* with Puddy and Elaine.

They arrived on the crowded deck and couldn't see anything. Leila mentally studied the position of the ship in comparison to the position of the life boats and said, "Let's just go back to our room and watch from our balcony, we'll get a much better view from there."

"Good idea, Mom," Zach said.

Taken aback at the compliment from her teenage son, she relished the praise as they quickly walked to their room. They entered their suite and immediately walked out onto the balcony. All of the life boats filled with corpses floated around the exterior of the floating dock system. Although the Disney Wonder didn't line the perimeter, they still viewed several life boats from their balcony. Each life boat/funeral pyre prepared to ignite and head out to sea away from the cruise ships.

A bugle blared, and *Taps* resonated throughout the ship. After a twenty-one-gun salute, Naval Officers wearing dress blues pushed all of the life boats out to sea. Once the boats floated safely away, the officers lit arrows, drew their bows and shot flaming arrows out onto the life boats and lit the pyres. Complete silence fell over the ship as everyone watched the flames rage as the boats floated away.

With the asteroid, Great Flood and massive funeral behind them, the survivors could begin to rebuild their lives and their civilization.

Sink The Zinc

Chapter Thirty-Six

122 days after first human dies of 61-DIVOC

Leila woke up the next morning with a new sense of hope. She firmly believed in the power of positive thinking, but today her optimism exploded. Sabbath jumped on top of her chest and kneaded her with alternating front paws, his way of marking her as his person. Then he gently batted her chin with his paw, his not so subtle hint to pet him. As Leila stroked his long black hair, Sabbath purred happily. *What a great way to wake up in the morning with a purring kitty.*

"You getting up, you lazy bum?" Luke asked as he exited the bathroom wearing a plush white towel wrapped around his waist.

"Are you crazy? I can't possibly disturb the royal highnesses." She nodded to a content Sabbath on her chest and to Mittens who slept on her feet.

Luke got dressed, walked into the kitchenette area and opened a can of cat food. Sabbath immediately jumped off of her chest and bolted to the kitchen. Mittens followed leisurely.

"You're evil," Leila scolded as she begrudgingly climbed out of bed. As she walked into the kitchenette area where all three kitties devoured their breakfast, the flat screen turned on.

President Ace appeared onscreen and said, "Greetings, My Fellow Americans. Our pilots flew all over the globe scouting for habitable land. All of the mountain ranges over twenty-five hundred feet tall are habitable. In fact, they remained unscathed because the water level only rose twenty-five-hundred feet."

Only rose twenty-five-hundred feet?

"Our East Coast jets scouted Europe, South America and Africa and East of the Mississippi while our West Coast jets scouted Asia, Canada and West of the Mississippi. Lots of habitable places exist around the world—Existing dwellings and structures along with plenty of buildable land. I'd like everyone to decide which mountain range you'd like to live on. Then we'll consolidate passengers to the appropriate cruise ships to efficiently sail the passengers to their final destination."

Leila squealed with delight. Her positive thinking really paid off today.

Ace continued, "Lots of wonderful mountain ranges to choose from. Dozens of ranges exist all over the United States and across the world, too. Too many to name, but there's a list scrolling across the bottom of your television screen. Thank you and God Bless America."

President Ace stepped away from the camera. The television stayed on and displayed a slide show of all of the mountain ranges around the world. Leila recognized many of them, but not all. Once the United States displayed all of its beautiful mountain ranges, the slide show displayed all of the European mountains. Many of them she'd never heard of, but some of them she'd actually visited. She recognized the Dolomites near Milan, Italy. During their Italian honeymoon, they'd seen just the mountain's tippy tops of the Dolomites from their train as it neared the station. But since the horrible weather offered nearly zero visibility, they decided to stay on the train, skip the Dolomites and travel straight to Milan.

The Alps pictures displayed next which covered many European countries including the Zugspitze in Germany. She recalled their trip to Germany for Christmas 2016 when the boys skied the Zugspitze on

Christmas Eve. Leila and Luke tried sledding which proved a lot harder than it looked. She'd even lost her white iPhone in the snow.

"Stop watching all the choices. You know exactly which mountain we'll live on," Luke said, then sipped espresso.

Agreeing with Luke, she knew exactly which mountain they'd live on.

Chapter Thirty-Seven

122 days after first human dies of 61-DIVOC

Leila's iPhone buzzed. Her brother started a group chat with their parents, even though her parents never texted in their lives. According to Mom, "They didn't have smart phones, they had dumb phones." The text read—*Family meeting in the main dining hall.*

Leila texted back—*Okie dokie. Give me an hour. I just got out of bed.*

"Who texted?" Luke asked.

"Damon called a family meeting in the dining hall," Leila said as she walked towards the bathroom to take a shower.

"He probably wants to discuss which mountain to live on." Luke followed her into the master bathroom.

Leila turned on the shower and took off her tank top and sleep shorts. After she tested the water, she stepped into the shower. "Shouldn't it be obvious to our family which mountain we'll live on?"

The Logan Family arrived at their usual table and their family greeted them. Niece Leila hugged her and gestured for her to sit at her usual seat. The Cast Member popped a bottle of champagne and poured everyone a glass, even her underage sons and nieces.

Leila raised her glass and toasted, "Here's to getting back onto dry land very soon."

"Cheers," everyone said in unison as they all clinked glasses.

After sipping champagne, Leila asked. "Who's going to live on Gateway Mountain with us?" Leila referred to their cabins in North Carolina. Although McMansions more accurately described their vacation homes. They'd built on top of Gateway Mountain in Old

Fort, North Carolina. They'd purchased adjacent lots thirteen years ago and built two homes which they cleverly rented out when not vacationing there.

"Do ya'll have enough room for all of us?" Damon asked.

"There's definitely more room than what we have now on this cruise ship," Leila quipped with an eyeroll. "The main house is over five thousand square feet if you count the apartment above the three-car garage. The guest house is just over three-thousand square feet. The mountain's elevation is about three-thousand feet. If the water level really rose twenty-five-hundred feet, we'll have a great mountain view *and* an ocean view."

"It'll seem more like a big hill," Luke said.

Euphoria filled her as a wonderful notion entered her brain. "Oh, my, God! Luke, are you thinking what I'm thinking?" Leila asked.

"Probably not. Because what I'm thinking shouldn't be said in front of our sons and parents." Luke winked, and everyone at the table laughed.

"All of our stuff at the tree houses should still be there!" Leila said excitedly. They'd nicknamed their nine-acre property the tree houses because gigantic trees filled the land and many of the exterior walls made with double-paned insulated glass offered the best views. Plus, the oversized windows maximized their views. Whenever they stayed there, they felt like they lived in a giant tree house.

Luke's eyes lit up, and she knew why.

Leila nodded and said, "The tree houses store half of our Armageddon supplies. We can live off the land there, too. In fact, one of my short stories, *Rutherfordium,* involved exactly that. Plus, I moved all of my precious photo albums to the tree houses because I always feared that they'd get ruined if a hurricane flooded our Florida home."

"Here's to the tree houses," Luke toasted.

Basking in the knowledge that their new lives would somewhat resemble their old ones, another realization struck her brain. Hundreds of people lived in mountain homes all over the world.

"There could be survivors!"

Chapter Thirty-Eight

125 days after first human dies of 61-DIVOC

It took three days to cruise to North Carolina. Passengers transferred amongst the various ships to sail the survivors to their mountain of choice. Luckily, the Logan Family stayed on the Disney Wonder.

Leila walked out onto the balcony for probably the last time. Impossible to believe, their cruise ship floated over what remained of North Carolina. It resembled cruising through icebergs near Alaska. Only instead of icebergs, mountain tops protruded through the water's surface.

"I hope this ship has good sonar," Leila said to Luke and the boys. Visions of the Titanic swam in her head. "Wouldn't it be ironic if the cruise ship struck a mountain top just below the water's surface."

"That's Grandfather Mountain." Zach pointed to the largest mountain on the horizon.

"We're close to our mountain. Is everything packed and ready to go?" Leila asked.

"Everything except for the kitties. We don't want to traumatize them anymore than necessary," David said as he cradled a sleepy Sabbath.

"The tree houses will be a bit crowded," Luke said.

"I think we should put the old people in the guest house and the rest of us can stay in the main house," Leila suggested.

"Mom, do the girls have to stay with us? They're so annoying," David whined.

"It's probably only temporary. Only about half of the home owners live on the mountain permanently. The other half mostly live in Florida. Certainly, they can find their own vacant house nearby," Leila said.

The ship steered its way through the peaks of mountain tops. Excitedly, Leila pointed. "Look, I see the Gateway Mountain sign. It's barely above water. That means that...."

Everyone looked up to search for the tree houses built on the same side of the mountain as the sign.

"I see the tree houses." Zach pointed.

"Oh, my, God. The tree houses still stand. Great eyesight, Zach. Good thing I made you eat your carrots growing up." Leila laughed.

Zach shrugged nonchalantly. "I saw the giant boulder on our property and knew the tree houses stood next to it."

"I see people." David pointed to a couple on the lower part of the mountain gawking at the cruise ship floating in their back yard.

"Yeah! Survivors!" Leila performed the sign of the cross.

"Uh, Mom. How will we get up to our tree houses?" David asked. "It's like five hundred feet above us."

"We're about to ride our first helicopter." Leila beamed.

"Yes." They boys fist bumped each other.

Knock, knock.

"That must be the Cast Members to load up all of our crap. Boys...."

"We know, Mom. Herd the cats," David said as he opened a carrier and shoved Sabbath in it.

Leila opened the door. Shock filled her as she stared at President Ace.

Chapter Thirty-Nine

125 days after first human dies of 61-DIVOC

"Mr. President. Won't you please come in." The Logan Family all shook President Ace's hand.

Several Secret Service Agents entered first and secured the suite before their beloved president entered.

"I wanted to say goodbye to the Logan Family," Ace said.

"All clear, Mr. President," a Secret Service Agent said.

"You honor us, Mr. President," Leila said.

"Nice hats, David and Zach." Ace acknowledged the boys' Keep America Great hats.

"Thank you, Mr. President," the boys said in unison.

"Which one is yours?" Ace asked as he stepped out onto the balcony and looked up at the mountain.

Luke pointed and said, "It's the two on the very top next to that giant boulder."

"Fantastic. That's a great house," Ace said.

"Thank you. Does this mean that you'll stay in North Carolina?" Leila asked.

"Actually, no. I'm staying on one of two ships directly over Washington, D.C. We'll run the country from a floating Whitehouse and Capitol Hill. The Vice President will stay on the other ship," Ace said.

"Where did most survivors choose to live?" Zach asked.

"Good question, young man. At least half wanted to stay in America. But many Americans with heritage from other countries wanted to live where their ancestors emigrated from. Asian Americans chose

Asia. Italian Americans chose Italy. German Americans chose Germany. You get the idea," he said.

Two Cast Members entered the suite and loaded their luggage and caged kitties onto two rolling luggage carts.

"Where will all the survivors live?" Leila asked.

"Many Americans have homes in the mountains, so they'll live there. Our Troops will go door to door to all of the homes in the mountains. If they're occupied, they'll move on to the next home. If it is empty, they'll let a family move in. In the meantime, they can continue to live on their respective cruise ships," he said.

"How much food did ya'll save on those cargo ships?" David asked. Leave it to a starving teenage boy to ask the President of the United States about food.

Ace patted David's back and said, "Don't worry, young man. No American will starve on my watch."

The Cast Members left the room with their luggage and precious kitties.

A Secret Service Agent held his hand to his earpiece, obviously listening to someone on their communication system.

"Mr. President, the helicopters arrived," the agent said.

"That's my cue. I enjoyed meeting all of you. I hope to see you again sometime," Ace said.

They all hugged President Ace and said, "Goodbye, Mr. President."

Ace walked to the entrance of the suite, and an agent opened the door for him. As he walked through the threshold, he turned around and said, "Finish that book, Leila. I want to know how it ends." Ace laughed at his own ironic humor.

Leila smiled and said, "Yes, Sir. One more thing, Mr. President. Please tell me. Was the virus real?"

President Ace said, "Of course not. The virus distracted everyone. The only good thing about the Fake News media is that people believe what they're told."

"One more question, Mr. President. Was the asteroid even real?" she asked.

President Ace asked, "What do you think?"

THE END

Author's Note

True events inspired *Sink The Zinc*. However, the conspiracy theories and global catastrophe are fictional. I wrote this book during the actual COVID-19 pandemic of 2020 as a way to cope with the uncertainty of our future and humanity as we know it. The timeline of my fictional 61-DIVOC virus, parallels the actual timeline of the Corona Virus up until April. In fact, if you turn this book upside down, you'll notice that my fictional virus is the upside-down and backwards version of the real virus—COVID-19.

The story of the Logan Family during this pandemic is inspired by true events. In fact, the happenings at home on a particular day align with the actual news events of the real pandemic. COVID-19 still plagued the world when I published *Sink the Zinc*. But my story ends in May because when I wrote the ending in April, I honestly thought this mess would be over by then. For years, my husband prepared for the Apocalypse. That's why I began the story nearly three years before the pandemic. Luckily, I lived long enough to finish writing *Sink the Zinc*. Hopefully, the Human Race will live long enough to read it. I literally wrote my own happy ending.

Terri Talley Venters,
Author of *Carbon Copy, Tin Roof, Silver Lining,
Luke's Lithium, Copper Cauldron, Cobalt Cauldron,
Calcium Cauldron, Chromium Cauldron, Zirconium
Cauldron, Sulfur Springs, Europium Gem Mine,
Noah's Nickel, Manganese Magic, Platinum Princess,
Plutonium Princess, Iron Curtains, Body Of Gold,
Under The Magic & Elements of Mystery*

Terri received her Bachelor's degree in Accounting, and Master's degree in Taxation from the University of Florida. She is a licensed CPA and a Second Degree Black Belt in Taekwondo. She lives on The Saint Johns River in Florida, with her husband, Garrison, and their two sons. Terri is currently writing *Under The Magic*. For more information about Terri's books, please visit her website www.ElementsOfMystery.com. Terri is the daughter of Leslie S. Talley, author of *Make Old Bones, Bred In The Bone, The Closer The Bone & The Bonnie, Bonnie Bone* which are also available at amazon.

Made in the USA
Columbia, SC
22 June 2023

18362949R00085